MURDER AT THE PAINTED LADY
Barbara Warren

Allie McGregor is thrilled when she inherits a Victorian mansion from her estranged aunt, Eliza Ramsdale. The mansion is one of Stony Point, Missouri's famous Painted Ladies, but the inheritance comes with strings attached. Eliza wants Allie to find the truth and clear the name of her husband, Otis Ramsdale, who died in prison. Allie accepts the challenge, but first she has to discover who is trying to drive her out of her new home.

Clay Carver just wants the job of restoring the Ramsdale house. He never planned on falling in love with the attractive new owner, but as the threats grow in intensity, Allie and Clay join forces to find the person behind the attacks. Can they stop the attacker before he or she goes too far?

MURDER AT THE PAINTED LADY

•

Barbara Warren

AVALON BOOKS
NEW YORK

Published by Avalon Books,
an imprint of Thomas Bouregy & Co., Inc.
160 Madison Avenue, New York, NY 10016

Library of Congress Cataloging-in-Publication Data

Warren, Barbara, 1934–
    Murder at the painted lady / Barbara Warren.
        p. cm.
    ISBN 978-0-8034-7653-0 (acid-free paper)   1. Nieces—
Fiction. 2. Inheritance and succession—Fiction.
3. Architecture, Victorian—Fiction.   4. Mansions—
Conservation and restoration—Fiction.   5. Family secrets—
Fiction.   6. False imprisonment—Fiction.
7. Missouri—Fiction   I. Title.
    PS3623.A8644M87 2011
    813'.6—dc22

                                    2010037160

PRINTED IN THE UNITED STATES OF AMERICA
ON ACID-FREE PAPER
BY RR DONNELLEY, BLOOMSBURG, PENNSYLVANIA

Dedicated to my family, who have always believed
in me and supported me. And a special thank you to
Lia Brown and Jennifer Graham at Avalon Books,
who have done such a great job. I also want to thank
my agent, Terry Burns. God bless you all.

Chapter One

Allie McGregor padded into the living room in her stocking feet to sort through the handful of mail she'd found in the box. Mostly bills, from the look of it. She hesitated at a legal-sized envelope from Bailey & Grant, Attorneys-at-Law. *Lawyers?* Why would they be writing to her? Three minutes later, she sat in a state of shock. She suddenly owned a Victorian mansion in Stony Point, Missouri. Her great-aunt Eliza Ramsdale, on her father's side of the family, had died, and Allie was her sole heir. She read the letter again, thinking there must be some mistake. All communication between her family and Aunt Eliza had broken off years ago.

Allie got to her feet and hurried into the bedroom to look for the family photo album, finally locating it in a corner of the closet. Back in the living room, she sat on the couch, thumbing through the pages until she found what she was looking for. Three years ago, she'd driven down to Stony Point to visit her great-aunt, in an attempt to mend family fences and curious about what had caused the problem in the first place.

She still smarted at the reception she'd received. Eliza had accused her of trying to worm her way in so she could "get everything I have," as she put it. She had refused to allow Allie to enter the house, insisting they talk outside on the wide front porch. But she *had* agreed to sit in the porch swing while Allie took her picture.

There she sat, frozen in place by the camera, frail, wizened, white hair growing sparse, her eyes as hard and direct as black diamonds. The Victorian-style house needed repairs, presenting a drab contrast to the painted and well-kept homes surrounding it. Allie stared dreamily at the picture. She'd always had an affinity for Victorian houses, and now she owned one. But even as her heart reeled with joy, her head stressed a different message. No matter how badly she wanted the house, she couldn't afford to keep it unless Aunt Eliza had also left her a ton of cash, which didn't seem likely. If she'd had very much money, she would have painted the house.

Something else bothered her. For as long as she could remember, all she'd heard about Eliza Ramsdale, which had been little enough, had suggested there was a mystery about the woman. Something only talked about in whispers. So why had Eliza remembered her in the will? There'd never been any contact between the two of them, and she certainly hadn't been made welcome on her one attempt to get acquainted. Was there a hidden reason for the bequest? She decided to ignore the flicker of unease prompted by the letter. All of that could be settled later. She owned Aunt Eliza's house, and for the time being that was enough.

The phone rang, and she absently reached for it. A voice, cold and abrupt, came over the line. "I hear you've inherited the Ramsdale house."

The words hit her like a dash of ice water. She'd just received the letter today. How could anyone else know about it? "Who is this?"

"No one you know. You don't have a right to that house, and if you're smart, you won't accept it."

Not accept it? He couldn't be serious. "Of course I'll accept it," she blurted. "My aunt left it to me."

"Eliza may have left it to you, but she just might have given you more trouble than you can handle too. You think about that, and you stay away from there."

Allie heard a click, followed by a dial tone. She replaced the receiver, surprised to notice that her hand was shaking. The night-blackened window acted like a mirror, throwing back her reflection. Anyone could be out there looking in. Leaping to her feet, she surged across the room to yank the curtains closed.

The house secured, Allie sank down into the bentwood rocker and picked up the letter, reading it once more. The house was hers. Aunt Eliza's lawyers said so. Would she let a threatening voice on the telephone scare her away? Not accepting her inheritance would be like receiving a present and then not being allowed to open it. She couldn't bear the thought.

She tried to put the call out of her mind, pretend it never happened, but she couldn't forget the menace in the man's voice. Concentrating on each word, she went back over everything he had said. *Eliza.* He'd called her that, so someone who knew her aunt—a friend or relative? Someone who thought he'd been cheated? That disembodied voice on the phone had been trying to scare her, make her afraid to accept the house. How far would the man go to stop her from taking possession?

Clay Carver leaned across the table, jabbing the air with a bread stick to make his point. "Look, Gilda, I want the job of restoring that house. Old Mrs. Ramsdale refused to even discuss it with me, but this niece might be more agreeable."

Gilda Latimer, receptionist for the Bailey & Grant law firm, shook her head. "Don't count on it. From what I've heard, she's planning on selling."

"Selling!" Clay put all the agony he felt at the idea into that one word. "She can't do that."

"Sure she can. She's got the buyers too."

"Already?" Clay pushed his plate of spaghetti to one side. "Who?"

"George Aiken for one."

"Aiken? The megadeveloper based in St. Louis? What does he want with it?"

"He says he wants to make it a weekend home."

Clay bit into a piece of bread smeared with roasted garlic and chewed thoughtfully. Let Aiken get his hands on the Ramsdale house, and Clay could kiss the restoration job good-bye. Aiken would bring in his own people.

"I wish I had the money—I'd buy it myself. When's this niece coming?"

"That I do know. She's due at the office at nine o'clock tomorrow morning."

"Okay, I'll be at the house, waiting. Get in on the ground floor, so to speak. Thanks, Gilda. I owe you."

"That you do, love. And I'll not let you forget it."

Twenty minutes later Clay left Gilda on her front porch and drove home, fighting a feeling of dissatisfaction. He'd wanted to restore the Ramsdale mansion ever since he'd gotten into the restoration business. There had been rumors about Eliza Ramsdale and her house, but rumors were rife in Stony Point. Most of the older homes had stories, real or exaggerated. Maybe there was more reason for gossip in the Ramsdale case, but people tended to hang loose here, and old Miss Eliza had been left to live in comparative solitude. Now that he had a shot at working on the Ramsdale place, he'd camp out on the front porch Monday morning until Allison McGregor showed up, and he'd do everything he could to persuade her to give him the job of restoring the house.

Allie drove the short distance between the Bailey & Grant law office and her great-aunt's home, quivering with anticipation. She'd spent a restless night, filled with troubled dreams. Now she tended to watch the rearview mirror more closely and scrutinize the side roads, making sure no one followed her or could take her unaware. Although she didn't have any idea what she could do if she suspected someone was stalking her.

The wrought-iron gate stood open, and she drove through, wondering who owned the red pickup parked in the driveway. She grimaced. After the cold fury of last night's phone call, coming here alone might have been a bad idea. A flash of movement drew her attention to the man who rose from the porch swing and strolled toward her. Broad shoulders filled his navy blue Windbreaker. Red hair glinted in the weak April sunlight. She reluctantly got out of the car, and he stopped about four feet away. His eyes were the deep indigo of a blue-bird's wing, but his expression was guarded.

"Miss McGregor? I'm Clay Carver. I heard you were coming today, and I was hoping to be able to speak with you." His hand gripped hers, strong, masculine, a bit rough, like that of a man used to hard work.

He heard she was coming? No one knew she was coming except her aunt's lawyer, so how did this man know her name, and what did he want? She jerked her hand away, a little too fast to be considered polite. "Where did you hear that?"

His smile faded. "From a friend. If you're planning to re-store the house, I'd like to have the job."

He held out a business card, and she automatically reached for it. *Carver's Construction. Restores and renovates antique buildings.* She let her gaze drift past him to the shabby old house, imagining it restored to a pristine condition, but it wouldn't happen on her watch.

She shook her head, reluctantly holding out the card. "I'm sorry. I love the house, but I can't afford to keep it, and even if I did, I don't have the money to restore it."

He ignored the card. "So you're going to sell?"

"I don't have a choice." Was he the person who had called her? No, probably not. Her caller had warned her not to come.

He shrugged. "Even if you plan to sell, think how much you'd increase the value of the house by restoring it. Probably double your money."

"Oh, well, probably so, but I can't afford it."

"I don't see how you can afford not to."

Allie gave him a frosty stare. "Well, perhaps we're coming at it from different perspectives. You'll excuse me?"

She turned away, looking up at the steeply pitched cross-gabled roof and the corner tower. If she could live here, that's where she'd have her bedroom. Imagine sleeping in a round room. She sighed. Wishing was easy. Making those wishes come true was the tough part.

A wide porch stretched across the front of the house, a

dilapidated swing the only furniture. The porch was the perfect spot for wicker chairs and pots of ferns, lazy summer afternoons, and moisture-beaded glasses of iced tea. She climbed the steps toward the frosted-glass panels of the paired entry doors, inserted the key, turned it, and stepped into the foyer. Oak paneling reached halfway up the walls. A soaring staircase dominated the small space, with a faded love seat and matching chairs arranged along each side. An elaborately carved table with a marble top held a bronze statue of Mercury.

"See what you have? How can you possibly sell it?"

Allie jerked around to find Clay Carver standing close behind her. He had followed her inside? What was wrong with this man? Didn't he understand the word *no*? "Look. I'm not interested in restoring anything at this time. I just want to look over my new house, if you don't mind."

"Not at all. Go right ahead," he said affably.

She glared at him, then walked away, aware that he followed. Should she be alarmed? She stopped in the kitchen and heaved an exasperated sigh when he entered right behind her.

"You'll want to modernize this, make it more efficient."

"How many times do I have to tell you, I can't afford to do anything? Read my lips. I do not have the money."

Voices coming from the front of the house interrupted them. A woman spoke with a loud note of authority. "Yes! I was right. We must purchase this house."

Allie shot Clay a questioning glance, then wheeled and strode toward the parlor. She stopped in the doorway, aware he was standing close behind her. A tall, heavyset woman with dark hair and a tight-lipped mouth slathered with bright red lipstick dominated the room. A shorter woman, her white hair pulled back in a bun, round, gold-framed glasses magnifying her blue eyes, seemed almost mouselike compared to the first female. They were standing in front of the fireplace, looking around as if they belonged there.

Allie cleared her throat, and their eyes met in the dusty mirror hanging over the mantel. The larger woman whirled, staring at her. "What are you doing here?"

Allie clamped down on a sudden spurt of anger. "I own this house. I think the question is what are *you* doing here?"

The woman raised her eyebrows, a haughty expression on her face. "My name is Maude Wheeler, and I am here to stake my claim on this property. I was told in a dream that this house should belong to me. Or to our group, I should say. Naturally, it would be in my name."

The smaller woman looked rebellious. "I'm sure you weren't told any such thing. You know the house should come to me. It's only right."

Allie interrupted them. "I'm sorry, but, as I said, the house belongs to me. I don't know what this is all about, but I'm afraid you'll have to leave."

"Mrs. Wheeler is the leader of a cult," a male voice said.

Allie turned to look at the man standing in the doorway, a tall, stern-faced figure. Someone important? Or just someone who thought he was important? And what was *he* doing here? Where had all these people come from, and what did they want? Had there been a notice in the paper? *Allie McGregor is in town. Go harass her.* She felt as if she was under siege.

"George Aiken here. Miss McGurdy, I presume."

"That's McGregor."

He ignored her correction, moving aside to allow a middle-aged woman wearing a red jacket over a navy and white dress to step past him.

"Miss McGregor? I'm Vista Harbuckle, owner of Harbuckle Realty. Mr. Aiken is interested in purchasing this house. We're prepared to make a deposit today."

"We'll meet any offer," George Aiken said. "Name your price. I need to get back to St. Louis for another appointment."

Allie bit back the terse remark she wanted to make. No matter how important this man thought he was, she found his brusque voice and impatient expression extremely irritating. She hadn't asked him to show up on her doorstep, and she resented his attitude.

Aiken flipped his keys against his hand. "My wife wants

this house, and what she wants, I see she gets. Come, come, Miss McGurdy. I'm a busy man."

"Now wait just a minute." Maude Wheeler shoved her way into the discussion. "I was here first. I believe my offer comes before yours."

"What offer?" he jeered. "A lot of mishmash about dreams. Junk. That stuff is just junk."

" 'Junk'?" Maude sounded as if she was about to choke over the word. She cleared her throat, her face a mottled red.

Clay's hands rested on Allie's shoulders as he gently moved her aside. "Miss McGregor is looking over the premises for the first time, so these offers are premature. I don't believe she's decided what she wants to do just yet."

"That right?" George Aiken demanded.

"I . . . yes. Of course."

Maude Wheeler opened her mouth, but Clay ignored her. "I believe you all should leave now and let her inspect the property. If she decides to sell, she can get in touch with you— Mrs. Wheeler at the bookstore, and you, Mr. Aiken, through Mrs. Harbuckle. That's right, isn't it?" He ushered them out, and Allie breathed a sigh of relief.

Maude Wheeler paused at the edge of the porch. "I'll be back." It sounded like a threat.

The smaller, white-haired woman stared at Allie, her expression grim. She seemed about to say something, but then she followed Maude down the steps. George Aiken strode to the sidewalk before turning and looking back, his face a blank mask. Allie tried to tell herself it was silly to feel threatened. These people, regardless of how strange they seemed, couldn't hurt her. But how did they know she'd be here today? And why did they all want Aunt Eliza's house?

Clay shut the front doors and grinned at Allie. "Well, that was quite a reception."

"How did they know I'd be here?" For that matter, how did he know? She'd found him on the front porch waiting for her, and she hadn't decided how she felt about that.

He shrugged. "Beats me. Aiken is a well-known speculator.

Buys up old estates, restores them, and sells for an inflated price."

"So he wouldn't keep the house if I sold to him?"

"Maybe not. I think his wife was a distant relation of Eliza's husband or something. Maude Wheeler and Mary Olson are members of some kind of a group. He's right on that. Maude runs a bookstore. I'm not sure what Mary does. I don't think she's from around here."

"They're rather strange, aren't they?"

He laughed. "Oh, Maude's all right, a little odd but harmless. I think she makes up the rules on what she believes as she goes along. She just likes to be important, and this is the way she goes about it. Don't worry. Most of the citizens here are solid. Don't judge the entire town by these three."

"What about Mrs. Harbuckle?"

"Vista's okay. She won't be a party to anything shady. As for the others, well, you get used to them."

"I guess so." She wasn't sure, though. "Why would all of those people want to buy the house?"

"I'd say that Maude wants to use it as a gathering place and probably plans to live in it. Restoring and living in the old Ramsdale house would lift her up a couple of rungs socially, I suppose. I've known her all my life. In fact, we grew up on the same street. As for Aiken, he probably sees it as an investment."

Not fully convinced, Allie nodded. She wasn't interested in bettering herself socially, but she wanted to live here so badly, she could feel the desire coursing through her like an electrical current. It would take all the emotional strength she had to turn her back and walk away.

Clay watched Allie as she looked around the room, her gaze lingering on the gold-framed mirror hanging over the fireplace. *Yes!* She wanted the house. Now, if only he could talk her into restoring it. Even if she had to sell it later, he could still use it as a stepping-stone to building a bigger business. He frowned. Gilda had told him when Allie would arrive. How had the others learned about it? Strange, they'd all shown up at the same time. Stony Point was a small town, and word got around, but it still left him feeling uncomfortable.

He followed Allie as she wandered from the parlor to the kitchen, her eyes shining with anticipation. Small and fragile, with long, silky, brown hair the color of chestnuts. Now she looked around the room, pausing to stroke the satin finish of the old oak table. It was easy to see she loved this house, and suddenly he wanted her to have it. Not just so he could restore it, but because she wanted it.

He took a mental step backward, surprised at the thought. Then he reconsidered. Yes, he'd like for someone who cared about the house to own it. The Ramsdale mansion had been one of the prettiest houses in town. It would be good for it to be a home again, lived in by someone who would take care of it. Old Miss Eliza never did anything toward keeping it up. Of course, maybe she couldn't afford to. He didn't know anything about Eliza Ramsdale's financial situation, but it bothered him to see a house like this falling on hard times.

Allie drove home, arguing with herself all the way. She wanted to live in her new house at least as long as she could, just to experience what it was like. By the time she reached home, she had almost convinced herself that moving in would be the smart thing to do. Look at the money she'd save by not having to pay rent, and she could probably find a job in Stony Point. There had to be some way she could live in that house and still make a living.

Once inside her apartment, she sat staring at the telephone for a good five minutes, trying to get up the nerve to call her aunt's lawyers. Finally, feeling she was burning her bridges behind her, she picked up the receiver and punched in the numbers. The receptionist answered on the first ring. Allie asked for John Bailey and soon had him on the line.

"Yes, Miss McGregor. What can I do for you?"

"I wanted to tell you I've decided to keep the house."

"Ah. And what caused this change of heart?"

"I've been thinking it over, and that's my decision."

"Well, I'm glad to hear it. Your aunt hoped you would. In that case, you need to come into the office to discuss an additional provision to your legacy. When would it be convenient for you?"

Allie thought. "Anytime, I guess."

"Say, tomorrow afternoon at two o'clock?"

"All right. I'll be there."

She hung up the phone feeling bewildered. *Another provision?* What was Bailey talking about? She thought he'd already told her everything. She still had her hand on the receiver when the phone rang.

"Miss McGurdy? George Aiken here. My lawyer is preparing a contract on the Ramsdale house. We need to reach an agreement on price."

Allie turned mulish. Despite her desperate financial situation, she would not be pushed around by this man. "I haven't agreed to sell yet."

"You will. Got a hunch you need the money."

"And you're planning to get a bargain—is that it?"

"Not at all. I'm willing to pay more than market value just to get this settled. I'm a busy man."

"Then don't let me keep you. No sale." Allie slammed down the receiver and spent a moment breathing deeply, striving to stay calm. The phone rang again, and she snatched it up. "Hello?"

"I'm not used to people hanging up on me, Miss McGurdy. Don't do it again."

She recoiled from the venom in his voice.

"Now, let's talk business."

She sensed that to show weakness would be a mistake. "No," she countered. "Let's talk about why you want the Ramsdale house so badly."

The hiss of a sharply drawn breath quivered over the line; then came the decisive click of a disconnected phone. George Aiken had hung up on her. Allie stared at the receiver she still held, feeling threatened in some way. Her caller last night had been a man who had known about her inheritance. George

Aiken had shown up this morning, determined to buy the house. Were they one and the same? Fear rippled through her. There were too many questions and not enough answers.

She looked around at her apartment, wanting to get away. Aunt Eliza had lived in the Ramsdale house. She could too. Pack a suitcase and leave early in the morning. She'd clean the tower and use it for her bedroom. Yes. That's what she'd do. Her confidence faded. So why did she feel like she was getting in over her head?

The phone rang, and Clay closed the book on Victorian houses he'd been reading, using a finger to mark his place. He lifted the receiver. "Yeah?"

Gilda Latimer's light laugh sounded in his ear. "That's not a very businesslike way to answer. What if I'd been a customer?"

"I'd have turned on the charm. No use wasting it on a bill collector."

"Practical man. I have news for you. Little Miss McGregor called. She's decided to keep the house."

"You're kidding. Does that mean she's going to restore it?" He was right. She couldn't sell once she'd seen it.

"I have no idea, darling. She does have some money coming if she keeps the house in the family, but I don't know how much."

Clay ignored the "darling." "Hmm. Miss Eliza didn't live very fancy. Wonder how much she had."

"Who knows? I don't have access to the financial records. She wouldn't be the first older person to die with a large sum of money hoarded in the bank."

"No, that's right. When's the McGregor woman coming back to town?"

"Tomorrow. She has a two o'clock appointment at the office."

"I see. Hey, thanks, Gilda. I owe you again."

"And someday I'm going to call in all those favors." She laughed, but there was a serious note in her voice.

Clay hung up the phone, wishing she wasn't so obviously interested. While he liked her, the excitement just wasn't there. He'd taken her out to dinner a few times, but there was nothing between them that promised more than friendship. It wasn't that he was afraid of commitment. In fact, he'd been knocking around for several years, and he'd like nothing better than to marry and settle down with the right woman. He just didn't think Gilda Latimer fit the description.

He placed a strip of paper in the book to hold his place and got to his feet. He'd walk past the Ramsdale house. Probably Allie McGregor still couldn't afford to restore it, but he just wanted to look it over. The house had a hold on him in some way. Other houses offered as much challenge, but none interested him like this one.

He shivered in the cool April air. Old-fashioned jonquils bloomed in the yards he passed, the bright yellow flowers coming earlier than the newer, larger varieties. The snowy blossoms of dogwood dotted the surrounding hills. A scent of frying meat drifted from a nearby house.

The Ramsdale place, when he reached it, was shrouded in darkness. It had a carriage house and a small guesthouse, as well as the main home. The large lot, surrounded by a decorative wrought-iron fence, was the perfect setting for a Victorian Painted Lady.

He leaned on the fence, picturing the house freshly painted, surrounded with beds of bright flowers. Rumors about the house and Miss Eliza were common knowledge. Otis Ramsdale, Eliza's husband, had died in prison. According to the tales, he was either an international jewel thief or just a homegrown one. There might have been something to the rumors, although he had his doubts, but if Otis had a cache of jewels, he'd taken the secret of their whereabouts with him. No one seemed to know what was supposed to have happened to his ill-gotten gains, although a lot of people seemed to think they might have an idea. He'd heard most of the rumors, but the last thing he was interested in was a tale of buried treasure. He just wanted to work on that house.

Clay stepped through the gate, walking on the soft grass. Something rustled in the old lilac hedge, probably a sleepy bird. He stared up at the tower room. Had he really seen a light, or had the brief golden glimmer been just a reflection of a distant car? He watched for a long time, but nothing more happened. Before leaving, he walked around the house looking for anything out of order, but everything seemed to be all right. Still, he left with a strong impression that someone had been inside the tower room.

Chapter Two

Allie drove the twisting road to Stony Point. The wrought-iron gate stood open, and she parked in the circular drive in front of the house. She got out of the car, listening to the muted sounds of traffic in the streets below. How could she have forgotten how isolated it was? A deep, wooded ravine marked the rear and the left boundaries of the lawn. The hillside dropped sharply on the right until only the roof of the neighboring house was visible through a thick band of trees.

She stared up at the shabby three-story house, which had been one of Stony Point's most prominent mansions in days past. Why had she ever thought she could live here by herself? She tightened her resolve. Maybe after a few nights it wouldn't seem so lonely.

The house was cool but not uncomfortable, making her wonder if the furnace was on. It would cost a fortune to heat this place. Fortunately, in a few weeks warmer weather would arrive, and she could forget gas bills. She could rough it until then if she had to.

Allie looked at the elegant statue of Mercury and almost pinched herself to see if she was dreaming. The house and everything in it belonged to her. She'd worn her oldest jeans and sweatshirt, planning to clean. Her appointment was at two, leaving her plenty of time to get some work done. She'd start in the kitchen.

One hour later she had a clean refrigerator and stove, and was standing on a chair wiping out kitchen cabinets when the doorbell rang. She climbed down and went to answer, hoping it wasn't those two irritating women again. It was a relief to see the broad shoulders and red hair of Clay Carver. At least he was normal.

Allie opened the door and smiled. "Good morning."

"Morning. I saw a car in the drive and thought I'd better investigate. Getting it cleaned up, I see."

She stepped back, holding the door open so he could come in. "Actually, I'm sort of between jobs, and since the rent was due on the apartment, and I owned this big house . . ." She spread her hands in a dramatic gesture. "Here I am."

He raised his eyebrows. "You're going to live here?"

"For now, anyway."

"What about doing some work on it?"

"Not unless someone gives me a good-sized chunk of money. I'm temporarily short of cash."

He shrugged. "If you decide to make any repairs, I'd appreciate it if you'd consider my company first."

"I'll do that." She smiled, wanting to give him a different answer. The house wouldn't seem so lonely with people underfoot working on it.

"Well, I'll let you get back to your cleaning. You still have my card?"

"I have it." She nodded, wishing there was some way she could get him to stay without being too obvious. The house was bigger than she remembered, the empty rooms echoing with silence. Having someone here with her would make it seem . . . friendlier.

Clay drove away from the Ramsdale house with mixed feelings. Gilda hadn't known when Allie would arrive, so he'd planned to keep dropping by, trying to catch her. He'd been lucky to find her at home on his first trip past.

He had an appointment today to make a bid to restore a Victorian cottage, and he needed the job, but his heart wasn't in it. He wanted to work on the Ramsdale house. He couldn't explain why he felt so drawn to that particular house, but he couldn't get it out of his mind. Seeing it restored to its original state was becoming an obsession.

For one thing, most of the houses in Stony Point had handkerchief-sized lots. The Ramsdale house was different. The way it sat back from the road, the large lot and surrounding trees, the graceful, old-fashioned lines fascinated him. He could visualize the house in its former glory—even knew the color of paint he thought it should have—and he wanted to be part of the work.

He remembered the light he'd thought he'd seen in the tower room and felt uneasy. Should he have mentioned it to Allie? She'd think he was crazy. He didn't really have anything definite to tell her, but he'd keep a watch on the house when he could. She'd looked small and vulnerable this morning, her eyes holding a hint of apprehension. Where she lived was none of his business, but he didn't like the idea of her staying there alone.

On an impulse Allie picked up the phone and called her parents. Her mother answered, and after the usual greetings, Allie blurted out, "Guess what."

"You've made up with Howard, and you're moving back home!"

Allie stopped, flustered by this unexpected answer. Made up with Howard? Not likely. "Well, no . . . that's not it."

"Oh, Allie, why not? He's such a nice young man."

In front of her parents, yes. In private moments he was cold and demanding. Tired of being treated like a none-too-bright stooge, she'd handed Howard, her fiancé of three years, his ring, packed up her pride, and left town.

"That's not why I called. Aunt Eliza died, and she left me her house."

"Eliza Ramsdale? I knew she'd died, but imagine her doing something like that."

Allie focused on the first part of that reply. "You knew she died? Did anyone in the family go to the funeral?"

"Why, no, I don't suppose they did. Why?"

"She was a relative." To Allie it seemed heartbreaking that not one family member had been there to say good-bye.

Her mother picked up on her meaning. "Well, I guess someone should have gone, but really, Allie, she had refused to have anything to do with the family for years. I doubt if she'd have wanted any of us."

"When I visited her, I received the impression she didn't like us very much. Why not?"

"I have no idea." Allie heard the reserve in her mother's voice and sensed a mystery. "Here's your father. Since it's his family, maybe he can tell you."

After a short pause her father came on the line. "What's this I hear about Aunt Eliza leaving you the house?"

"She really did, Dad. Imagine that."

"Hard to believe. The way she hated the whole family, and then to go and do that."

"Why did she feel that way toward us?" She couldn't bring herself to use the word *hate.*

"I don't really know."

Allie sensed he was trying to avoid a direct answer. "I'm listening. Come on, Dad, tell."

She could almost see him shrug. He hesitated, and when he spoke, she felt he was choosing his words carefully. "The way I heard it, Otis Ramsdale got into some serious trouble, and instead of rallying around, the family basically disowned him. I guess that upset Eliza."

"Why would they do that?" The McGregors weren't perfect, but they did stand by family.

"I haven't a clue, Allie. I supposed I never cared enough to ask."

"What kind of trouble?"

"I'm not sure. Something serious, or the family wouldn't have turned on him like that."

What about Eliza? Had the trouble been bad enough to cause the McGregors to reject one of their own? Or had Eliza been involved too? "Did you ever meet her?"

"A long time ago. Now that I think about it, there were some rumors concerning the Ramsdale place. Something tied to Otis' trouble. I don't know why old Eliza left you that house, but maybe you hadn't ought to get involved with it."

"Oh, Dad. It's just a house. What harm can there be in accepting it?"

"None, I guess." He didn't sound convinced. "But I'd rather you didn't. I don't think I'd want you involved in anything concerning the Ramsdales. They're not our kind of people."

"They're both dead. What harm can they do now?" And what was this about *our kind of people*? Her father wasn't a snob, dividing people into *our kind* and *not our kind*. Was there something about Eliza and her house he wasn't telling her?

"Otis still has family somewhere, if they're not all in jail. I don't like you doing this, Allie, but I can see you're determined. You be careful."

"I will. I promise."

"Any message for Howard?"

"None."

She hung up the phone before he could protest. Whatever the problem between Aunt Eliza and her McGregor kin, it had nothing to with her, but she still couldn't help wondering. Maybe she could at least find out what Otis had done.

She didn't like Howard keeping in close touch with her parents. When she returned his ring, she had supposed his conceit would prevent him from trying to talk her into coming back. It looked as if she'd been mistaken. That overweening pride of his probably wouldn't let him admit she'd thrown him over. Well, his gofer girl had freed herself, and she had no intention of allowing him to order her around again.

A little squiggle of worry intruded on her thoughts. Her father had always been overly protective where she was concerned, but something in his comments about the Ramsdale house sounded more serious than his usual fatherly admonitions. She pushed the thought away. It was just a house, and for a little while at least, it belonged to her. She couldn't pass up a chance to explore it, and who knew what treasures she would find?

At 1:30 Allie cleared away the remains of her light lunch and drove to the office of Bailey & Grant. A faint little quiver of anxiety tingled in her stomach as she wondered what sort of revelation waited for her. Was the house not hers after all? No, Mr. Bailey had seemed glad she planned to keep it. She parked in front of the office and went inside. Gilda Latimer turned from her computer and smiled, but Allie sensed a calculating look behind the friendly expression.

"Good afternoon, Miss McGregor. I'll tell Mr. Bailey you're here."

She was back almost immediately, motioning for Allie to follow. "He'll see you now."

John Bailey was seated behind his desk: short, a little plump, white hair, bushy white eyebrows, and a friendly smile. "Miss McGregor. I trust you had a good trip down?"

"Oh, yes. I came early and did some cleaning at the house." She sat down across the desk from him, holding her purse in her lap. Mr. Bailey seemed oblivious to the worry she was sure shone in her eyes. He couldn't take the house away from her now. He just couldn't.

The lawyer shuffled through some pages on his desk. "I suppose you're wondering why I asked you to come here today."

"Well, yes." She couldn't say more.

He evidently found the page he wanted. "Your great-aunt had some rather odd ideas." He stopped, as if giving her a chance to respond. When she didn't say anything, he continued.

"She left you the house with no strings."

Allie sagged with relief. The house was hers. She had worried for nothing.

"If you had decided to sell it, that's all you would have received."

She frowned at him, not understanding where he was going with this. "Excuse me?"

"There was another bequest, and I tried to talk her out of

wording it this way, but she was adamant." Mr. Bailey placed the sheet of paper on his desk and folded his hands. "Well, to make a long story short, she left you seventy-five thousand, which you could only receive if you decided to keep the house. If you had sold, the way you originally planned, the money would have gone to the local SPCA."

Allie gaped at him. "How much?"

He frowned at her, probably thinking she was too scatter-brained to handle an inheritance. "Seventy-five thousand."

"Dollars?" She wanted to be clear on this.

He nodded.

Allie opened her mouth, closed it, and then opened it again. "If she had that much money, why didn't she have the place painted?"

Mr. Bailey looked as if he'd just bitten into a lemon. He hesitated, then said, "I don't make a habit of talking about clients, but I suppose you have a right to ask questions. Mrs. Ramsdale was rather economical."

"You mean *tight*?" Allie asked.

He nodded, a pained expression crossing his face.

"Have you seen the condition of that house?" she demanded.

Mr. Bailey unbent a little. "Precisely. But she said she wouldn't need it much longer, so why should she put up with a bunch of strangers tramping around in the way, making repairs she could get by without?"

"I guess that's one way of looking at it. Why did she leave it to me?"

"You came to see her."

"But she didn't want me. She wouldn't even let me inside the house."

"Mrs. Ramsdale was a complex woman. I believe she had a grudge against her husband's family."

"She didn't get along with her own family either. Although I don't suppose the McGregors did much to endear themselves to her." She suspected the problem had originated on both sides.

"You came. No one else ever did. I think she felt she had to leave her possessions to someone. She made the new will the day after you visited her. She may have had another reason, but if so, I'm not aware of it."

"I see." Allie said. "That's so sad."

"Yes," he agreed. "She was a sad woman. I'll make arrangements with the bank. The money's yours."

Allie shook her head in amazement. "I never expected anything like this. I'm overwhelmed."

"I can understand that, but if there is anything I can do to help you, let me know."

Allie thanked him and left, feeling that things were definitely picking up. She was rich. Well, maybe not rich, but she had more money than she'd ever seen before. She'd talk to Clay and have him estimate the cost of painting the house. Maybe she could make do with that and cleaning up the inside. She knew exactly what she wanted to do. She was going to open a bed-and-breakfast.

She drove back to the house, thinking Mr. Bailey's theory about Aunt Eliza had been right, as far as it went. She still had an uneasy feeling that there was more to her inheritance than met the eye. Sure, she'd come to visit, but that wasn't a good enough reason for leaving her such a generous gift. She had a sense of waiting for the other shoe to drop. Like maybe she was riding into an ambush.

She got out of the car and climbed the steps. A nine-by-twelve brown envelope with her name written on it lay in front of the door. Allie bent to pick it up, wondering what it could be. She gingerly slid a hand inside and pulled out a piece of paper. It took a minute to realize what she held. *Eliza K. Ramsdale, 86, Stony Point, Missouri, passed away. . . .* Someone had left her a copy of Aunt Eliza's obituary.

The clipping fluttered from Allie's fingers to the porch floor. She hesitated, then bent over and picked it up, suspecting that whoever had done this was trying to conduct a war of nerves. Probably the clipping was related to the phone call, trying to scare her into leaving. Well, she wasn't running. Here she was, and here she planned to stay.

She left the newspaper clipping lying on the kitchen table and spent the next hour and a half cleaning the tower so she would have someplace to sleep. The room evidently hadn't been used for a bedroom, since the only furniture was a rocker and a long oak table. No problem, though. She'd just wander through the house looking for something she liked. The bedrooms were completely furnished, and a quick glance into the attic rooms showed more items stowed away up there.

Allie found a wonderful, ornate brass bed with a high headboard and a low foot rail. A small round table would hold a bedside lamp with a pedestal base and a frosted globe. A mahogany vanity and matching chest of drawers would be enough for now. All she had to do was get them moved to the tower room. She trudged downstairs and dug Clay Carver's card out of her purse. He answered on the second ring. The deep timbre of his voice reached out to her over the phone line.

"Mr. Carver, this is Allie McGregor."

"Well, hello there. Good to hear from you."

"I want to ask you for a favor." She heard the hesitation in her voice, but if Clay noticed, he didn't give any sign.

"Sure, what can I do for you?"

"Well, it seems that I do have a little money after all, and perhaps I can do some work, like painting the house, and I wondered if you were still interested."

"You bet I am." She smiled at the enthusiasm in his voice. "I'll stop by with paint samples, and we can talk about it."

"There's something else." How could she ask him to do this? She hardly knew him. But she didn't know how she could manage without his help. "I need some furniture moved into the tower room. I've decided to sleep there."

"Oh . . . sure. When did you want it done?"

"Well—like, now?" She heard a gusty sigh, then silence. "If you don't have time, that's all right."

"No, I'm thinking."

She waited.

"Okay. I'll get a couple of guys to help and be right over."

55089

"You don't have to—" she began, but he interrupted.

"That's fine. I want to go over the house anyway and make a list of what needs to be done."

"All right, if it's not too much trouble." Allie hung up the phone and prowled through the rooms to see what else she wanted. A picture of a storm raging around a lighthouse appealed to her, and she found a low bookcase that would fit along one wall. A wing chair and footstool were added to her list, and as an afterthought she chose an empty, flat-topped steamer trunk to use as a table at the foot of the bed.

She was standing by the window looking out when Clay's pickup entered the drive, followed by a bronze minivan. By the time the doorbell rang, she was at the foot of the steps, ready to answer. The two guys with Clay were pleasant, but she felt overwhelmed at first with three large men in her narrow foyer.

Tom, the dark-haired one with a mustache, glanced admiringly around the space. "Would you look at that paneling? And it's in original condition."

"That's the good part," Clay said. "Miss Eliza didn't do any remodeling or painting. What you see is the real thing. Check out the floor."

The sandy-haired man grinned. "These two can go on for hours about woodwork. I'm a car man myself. Adam Harris, Miss McGregor. Where's that furniture you need moved?"

She led the way upstairs to point out the items she wanted, and they got to work. The tower room had been swept and mopped. The windows glistened in the April sunlight. With the furniture in place, it looked bright and homey. Allie surveyed it with pride. She could sleep here and not be afraid.

Tom and Adam left in the minivan, and Clay followed Allie to the kitchen, where he opened his notebook and fished for a pen. She felt the familiar squiggle of worry. "This is going to be really expensive, isn't it?"

Clay got a cautious look. "Yeah, it probably will be."

Allie sighed. "I guess I'll need to go ahead with it. I'm thinking of opening a bed-and-breakfast."

He was silent for minute, looking surprised. "Well, yes, you could do that."

"I can't afford to live here unless I come up with a way to make a living."

"I understand. I just hadn't gotten past the restoration part."

Allie reached for a notepad. "I'll need more than one bathroom."

"And probably you'll want some soundproofing."

"I will?" She hadn't thought of that. "Will that be expensive?"

"It will cost. Tell you what. Let me look over the house and make a list of what you need. Then we can decide which is the most important and work our way down."

She liked the way he'd said *we*. Probably he didn't mean anything by it, but it sounded good. She didn't feel so alone. She had an uncomfortable feeling she was beginning to depend too much on Clay Carver. Her problems weren't his responsibility, and she needed to be careful not to impose.

Clay closed his notebook, which made the obituary flutter. He picked it up. "What's this?"

"I found it on the porch in that envelope."

"The envelope has your name written on it."

"Yes. Who do you think could have left it there?"

Clay read the clipping. "I think the question is, why? What could they hope to accomplish?"

Allie stared out the window, not wanting him to see the distress she was sure shone in her eyes. "A lot of people seem to want this house."

"And this is supposed to drive you out? Rather weak attempt, if you ask me."

Add it to the phone call he didn't know about, and all of the people who were demanding she sell them the house, and it didn't seem all that weak to her. She didn't say so, because she still didn't know whom to trust. She hoped Clay was all right, but she needed to remember he had an agenda too.

She hesitated. "Clay, how did Aunt Eliza die?"

He stared at her. "I don't know. She was old, Allie. I imagine her heart just played out. Why?"

"I just wondered if there was a message behind the obituary being left here, a threat of some kind."

Clay shook his head. "Don't even go there. You'll just scare yourself for no good reason. No one killed Miss Eliza, if that's what you're thinking. I'd stake my life on that."

"No, I suppose not. I was just trying to make sense out of it. Why leave an obituary?" But in spite of his reassuring words, she couldn't help thinking that it just might be her life being staked on that premise. What if he was wrong?

Clay shrugged. "Who knows? I'd not worry too much about it, if I were you. Probably just someone playing a prank." He packed up his notes. "I'll be back in the morning to go over the house, if that's all right."

Allie followed him to the door and watched as he drove away. The stillness of the house settled around her. Had Aunt Eliza ever felt afraid when she lived here? She wandered out to the guesthouse at the rear of the property, which consisted of a living room, bedroom, bath, and kitchen. Small and compact, but it could be made cozy. Maybe she could fix this up and rent it too.

Not wanting to start any major cleaning jobs this late in the day, and wanting to get away from the house, she decided to take a walk. Grass was starting to green. Spring bulbs sent slender spikes of foliage through the cold ground. A clump of snowdrops brought her to a stop. Her grandmother had raised snowdrops. Maybe she could plant some bulbs this fall. She was a homeowner now. The glow lasted until she thought about insurance and taxes and repair bills. Her legacy wouldn't last long. She had to make the bed-and-breakfast work, or she couldn't keep the house. She stopped to admire a small concrete fawn resting on a low stone wall. A woman who had been raking leaves smiled at her.

Allie smiled back. "I was admiring your fawn. He looks almost real."

The woman rested her hand on the little gray statue. "He's been here for as long as I can remember."

The fawn had been formed with his legs tucked under him. Its sightless eyes seemed to stare serenely past them. Allie felt a sudden longing, probably caused by the realization that he was out of her reach.

"I was going to ask where you got him, but if he's that old, I'd guess none would be available."

"I'd say not," the woman said. "Do you live in Stony Point?"

"I do now. I'm Allie McGregor, and I inherited the Ramsdale house."

"Miss Eliza's place? I'm Cora Witner. I liked Eliza."

"You knew my aunt?"

"Practically everyone in Stony Point knew Miss Eliza."

Cora looked to be in her late thirties. She wore her dark hair cut short like a pixie's, and long, dark lashes framed her warm brown eyes. Although they were strangers, something clicked between them. Allie liked her immediately.

Cora glanced over her shoulder at the white two-story frame house behind her. "I live here with my father. He's very ill." Her expression clouded. "In fact, he's failing fast. The doctors say there's nothing more they can do for him."

"Oh, I'm so sorry. Can I do anything to help?" She knew the offer was worthless. Of course there was nothing she could do for this friendly woman with the worried expression.

Cora seemed to appreciate her concern, although she shook her head. "No one can do anything for him . . . or for me."

Before Allie could ask what she meant, Cora picked up her rake. "I'd better go check on him. He was asleep, and I needed some fresh air, but I don't leave him for long."

"I understand."

Cora started to walk away, then turned back. "Welcome to Stony Point, Allie. I hope you'll be very happy here."

"Thank you. Perhaps we'll see each other again."

A strange expression crossed Cora's face, almost as if she was angry about something. "Perhaps so. Who knows?"

She turned without another word and walked toward the house, leaving Allie to stare after her. What had gone wrong? One minute they were getting along fine, and then it was as if something had happened to upset the other woman, but Allie had no idea what.

Chapter Three

Before it got dark, Allie carefully locked all the doors and checked the windows. Satisfied the house was secure, she climbed the stairs to the tower room, carrying a milk-glass compote she had decided to put in one of the bedrooms. The one bathroom on the second floor was adequate but not fancy. The old claw-footed tub had been on her list of discards, but after stretching out full length and resting her head against the porcelain back while lavender-scented water lapped her chin, she changed her mind. Okay, the tub stayed.

The phone rang, and, with a towel wrapped around her, she hurried downstairs to answer. As soon as she could, she'd have a telephone put in upstairs in her bedroom. She spoke into the receiver, expecting one of her parents to be on the line, checking on her safety. Instead she heard nothing. Total silence. Then a harsh voice spit out the words, "I told you to stay away. If you're smart, you'll get out."

A click signaled that the caller had hung up before she could find words to answer. Her breath caught in her throat. An icy chill enveloped her, like a sudden draft. Alone in this huge, empty house, she felt vulnerable. Who was tormenting her like this?

Later, in her second-story bedroom with the windows bared to the stars, she felt . . . well, she didn't know how she felt. She listened to the silence, straining to hear something . . . anything. Never had she been so wide-awake. She stood it for as long as she could, but the everlasting quiet got to her. It was a long time before she could go to sleep.

28

all right, but he could tell from the set of her chin that she had no intention of talking about it.

He left thinking that, despite her protestations to the contrary, Allie McGregor gave a good imitation of a frightened woman. The thought disturbed him, more than he cared to admit. All he wanted from Allie was a restoration job. She was practically a stranger. Nothing to him on a personal level. But he found himself reliving their conversation, looking for clues as to what could have disturbed her. It wasn't anything to him, but she didn't have any business living in that big house by herself.

Allie saw Clay out and closed the door behind him. He hadn't paid any attention to the bowl, but he *had* asked her twice if anything was wrong. Had he picked up on her fear, or did he know something about the bowl's being moved? But how could Clay, or anyone else, get in? She'd kept the key in her possession since receiving it at the lawyer's office.

Allie glanced around the foyer, thinking of the list of chores she needed to accomplish today before deciding she wasn't in the mood to clean. Time to take a break. She went upstairs for her handbag and car keys.

The downtown streets were relatively quiet, and she enjoyed just strolling through the area. She stopped in front of a bookstore, thinking maybe she could get a book on Painted Ladies. Inside she roamed the aisles, reading the titles.

"What are you doing here?" an acid voice boomed from behind her.

Allie whirled, dropping the volume she had just lifted from the shelf. One hand flew to her throat. "What . . ."

Maude Wheeler didn't bother to apologize. In fact, from her expression, she seemed to feel that Allie was in the wrong. "I asked you a question. What are you doing in my shop?"

"I . . . well . . . I was looking for a book," Allie stuttered. Why did she let this woman shatter her wits like this?

"Oh?" Maude's eyebrows arched. "And just what kind of book are you looking for?"

"A book about Victorian houses," Allie gasped, wishing she had never ventured into this store. Maude was big-boned, heavyset, and angry. Not a good combination. Her harsh, authoritative voice overrode any protests.

"Why would you want such a book? I've heard what you're doing to my house. How dare you turn it into a bed-and-breakfast? You must stop this desecration at once."

Allie latched on to one part of this harangue. "*Your* house? My aunt left it to me."

"That deceitful, wicked woman did a terrible thing. And you are an interloper intruding where you have no business being. Leave my establishment at once."

Allie stared at her in confusion. The woman was throwing her out of this tacky bookstore? Just who did she think she was?

Maude whipped herself erect, arm extended, forefinger aimed at the door. "Go. I say, go!"

Allie whirled, plunging toward the door. What had she gotten herself into?

She was disappointed when she reached home and Clay's pickup wasn't parked in her driveway. Not that she wanted to see him or anything. Still, he was a *normal* person compared to some of the others she'd met. And she needed a dose of normal right now.

The minute she entered the kitchen, she knew someone had been in the house. The milk-glass bowl was back on the table, but now it held oranges and bunches of large black grapes. The hair on the back of her neck prickled. Her ears strained against the oppressive silence, but she heard nothing. Her emotions ran from fear to rage. This was her house, and whoever was playing their tricks had better stop. She was not going to be driven from her home by childish pranks.

She grabbed a broom and marched through the house, room by room, bent on flushing out any intruders who might be hiding. Every outside door was locked, and no one lurked in any of the rooms, nor the attic. No one was there, but someone had been.

Allie fled to the kitchen, where she found the phone book and let her fingers walk through the yellow pages until she stopped at Hayes and Sons, locksmiths. Bob Hayes promised to come the next day and change the locks on every door. If someone had used a key to prowl the rooms and move things around, then he was in for a surprise. *Or she,* Allie amended, remembering Maude Wheeler's arrogant claim that she should be living in the Ramsdale house.

She hung up the phone, feeling better, and went back upstairs. Today she would look through the rooms, planning how to furnish each. The restoration project would be expensive. She'd have to do as much decorating herself as possible. Fortunately, there was a lot of furniture to choose from. Maybe she could sell some items and use the money for wallpaper and paint.

She was standing in the middle of the right front bedroom, planning the color scheme, when she heard the music. The tune was an old one her grandmother used to sing. Her mind formed the words. *"Let me call you sweetheart, I'm in love with you."*

Allie stepped out into the hallway, listening. The music drifted through the air, seemingly taunting her. *"Let me hear you whisper that you love me too."* She ran for the staircase. Before she reached the attic, the music stopped, cutting off the tinny voice in midnote. The silence had a waiting quality. Allie froze, one foot planted on the next step.

She had just checked the attic. No one was there; she'd take an oath on that. No one human. She whirled, stumbling down the steps, not stopping until she reached the first floor.

Clay arrived at the Ramsdale house at two thirty. He'd meant to get there sooner, but things had come up. The paint had been ordered and would be delivered in a couple of days, but before they could start painting, the outside had to be scraped and the house prepared for the new color. He was so eager to get started, you'd think he was going to live there. His crew would arrive when they finished what they were working on now, but he couldn't wait. He wanted to start scraping this afternoon.

He parked in front of the old Victorian mansion. When Allie answered the door, he thought she looked scared. "What's wrong?"

She shook her head. "Nothing."

Her eyes were darkened pools set in a white face. Something had upset her, all right, but she was too stubborn to tell him anything. He stared down at her while a red flush stained her cheeks. Okay, he'd let it go for now. Maybe someday she'd trust him, but evidently she hadn't reached that place yet.

"I thought I'd get an early start on scraping the house. How about a cup of coffee before I begin?"

He thought she looked relieved, but she didn't say anything, just turned and headed for the kitchen. He followed, looking around to see if he could spot anything out of order. The white bowl he'd seen that morning was now filled with oranges and grapes.

"Been to the market, I see."

She reached up into the cabinet for a cup. "No."

He stared at her back. That was it, just *no*? She wasn't wasting any words today. "Where did you get the fruit, then?"

She poured coffee into two mugs, placing one in front of him. "I have no idea."

"Huh?"

She sat down across from him, and he took a deep breath and started over. "I mean—what are you talking about?" Which wasn't a whole lot better.

She didn't say anything for a moment; then she pressed her lips together and sort of nodded her head as if she'd made a decision. He waited, sensing something important here. She looked directly at him, and his heart constricted. She *was* scared. He didn't want anything frightening her. She might decide not to do any work on the house.

"I'm beginning to think I'm losing my mind," she said.

He shook his head. "You're all right. Just tell me what's wrong, and I'll take care of it."

"I'm not sure you can. This is going to sound strange." Her voice held a warning note.

He tried to grin. "Don't worry, I can take it."

She sighed. "Last night when I went to bed, that bowl was in one of the bedrooms on the second floor. This morning it was sitting in the middle of the kitchen table. I placed it over on the counter and went downtown for a while. When I returned, it was back on the table, but this time it was full of fruit."

"Who has a key to the house?"

"No one that I know of, but then, I wouldn't. The attorneys gave me a key, but maybe there was an extra one somewhere. I have no idea how many Aunt Eliza handed out."

"Not many, I'd guess," Clay said. "She wasn't all that trusting or that friendly either."

"That's not all," Allie said. "I was upstairs just now, and I heard music."

"What kind of music?"

"An old song, 'Let Me Call You Sweetheart.' Not something anyone would play in this day and age."

"No, I'd guess not. I'll take a look."

"I looked earlier when I found the bowl and fruit. There was no one in the house."

"There had to be." Otherwise this was beginning to sound like ghosts, and he didn't believe dead people hung around to haunt a house.

But Allie was shaking her head. "No. I would swear no one was here."

"That's impossible."

Her voice cooled. "I didn't think you'd believe me. If you'll excuse me, I have work to do."

She rose from her chair, but he reached out and caught her wrist. "I believe you, but you have to admit, it sounds sort of strange."

"I know exactly how it sounds, but I'm telling the truth."

The doorbell rang, and she left to answer. He trailed along to find George Aiken and a tall, auburn-haired woman Aiken introduced as Renata, his wife. Allie looked flustered, but she led them into the front parlor and offered to bring coffee.

They sat down, but Aiken shook his head and held up a

hand to stop her. "We don't have that long. My wife wanted to look over the house to see what changes she wants to make."

Clay watched as Allie stiffened. "Why would your wife want to make changes to my house?"

"Because I'm going to buy it for her." He took out his checkbook. "I've run a background search on you, and you're broke. You can't afford to keep up this place. I'm prepared to offer you more than it's worth to take if off your hands. Renata gets the house she wants, and you get enough money that you won't have to work for a long time."

Clay held his breath as a thoughtful expression slid across Allie's face, but then she tilted her chin and stood a little taller. "I've told you several times, the house is not for sale."

"Now look here, young lady. . . ."

She interrupted him, which, judging by the expression on his face, just didn't happen to George H. Aiken. "I've asked you this before, but now let me rephrase it. Why does your wife want this house so badly?"

Renata spoke for the first time, her voice a haughty drawl. "I am a great-niece of Otis Ramsdale. By all rights this house should have come to me anyway."

"Oh, yes?" Allie's eyes glowed, and Clay figured she was getting ready to let fly. Before he could rush to head her off, it was already too late.

"I would like to point out that your uncle died before my aunt, which means the property belonged to her, and she had a right to leave it to anyone she pleased."

Renata flushed. "I can't believe she would pass over us for a stranger."

"Oh? You visited her often?" Allie asked, her voice dangerously still.

"Well, I don't know as you'd say often. . . ." Renata said, as if not sure how to answer.

Clay grinned. She was probably wondering how much Allie knew. He'd bet George and Renata hadn't spent much time in Stony Point, let alone at Miss Eliza's.

"How often?" Allie demanded. "It's easy to check, you know. All I have to do is ask some of her friends, and I can probably get a detailed list of when you came and when you left."

Renata gave in. "All right, then. We never visited. But that doesn't change the fact that my uncle bought and paid for this house, and it should be mine."

"Miss McGregor has decided not to sell," Clay said, thinking Allie needed help, although to give the lady credit, she seemed to be holding her own.

"We could contest the will," Aiken threatened.

"You could," Clay agreed. "I don't think you'd get anywhere with it, though. After all, Otis has been dead for several years, and Eliza was the sole owner. She had a right to do what she wanted with the property."

Aiken frowned. "Very well, but this isn't the last of it. I'll talk to my lawyer."

"You do that," Clay said. "I believe Miss McGregor's attorney is John Bailey. You can direct all correspondence to him."

Renata shot him a look of acute dislike.

Allie stood with one hand resting possessively on a dark blue upholstered wing chair, looking every inch the lady of the house. He was proud of her.

"Mr. Carver has told you the truth," she said. "This house is not for sale. Now will you please leave? And if you have anything further to say, you may talk to my attorney."

George Aiken got to his feet. "I don't like being blocked in what I want, and I want this house."

"We don't always get what we want," Allie said. "Good-bye, Mr. Aiken."

George and Renata left in a huff, and Clay shut the door behind them. When he got back to the parlor, Allie had slumped in the wing chair, looking as if she was going to cry. He knelt down in front of her.

"Hey. They're gone. You did a great job of handling them."

She gripped his arm. "I'm glad you were here. Clay, why do so many people want this house all of a sudden?"

"I guess it's not as sudden as all that. No one could get it while Miss Eliza was alive. Now she's gone, and they're crawling out of the woodwork."

"But why?"

He hesitated, then decided to go ahead and tell her. She'd hear it somewhere anyway. "What do you know of your great-uncle Otis?"

"Not much. My family never talked about him."

"The way I get it, he wasn't anything to brag about. You see, ol' Otis was a jewel thief. A pretty good one, from what I hear."

"A thief?" Allie stared at him, wide-eyed. "Aunt Eliza's husband was a thief?"

"That's what they say. Stony Point was a pretty important place in its time. A lot of rich people lived here. Where you have rich people, you have jewels."

"He *stole* them?"

"And apparently got away with it for a while. He took Eliza on cruises overseas, and there were rich people on the boats and at the parties they were invited to. He always had money, and he spent it."

"I suppose he got caught."

"They always do." He was glad to see a little color coming back into her cheeks "There was a trial, and he went to prison. Died there from a ruptured appendix a few years later. I guess it turned Eliza bitter. She didn't have much to do with people after that."

"Do you think she knew?"

"I don't know. I doubt if anyone does. It happened a long time ago." He hoped he'd distracted her for the time being, but she was too smart for him.

She raised her eyes to meet his. "That still doesn't explain why everyone wants the house."

He grinned. "Well, seems they never found all the jewelry. A lot of people think it's hidden here."

He could almost see the wheels turning in her head. "Who would the jewels belong to now?"

He shrugged. "The insurance company, I suppose, if you were being honest about it."

"And if you weren't?"

"I guess there are places you could sell them. I wouldn't know about that."

She looked at him, and he felt a tremor of warning. "Why do you want to restore the house?" she asked.

He stared at her in dismay. "You think I'm after the jewels?"

"I don't know you very well."

"I don't know you very well, either, but I don't suspect you of trying to find your uncle's hidden loot so you can sell it on the black market." Was that what she thought of him? For two cents he'd walk out right now. The stricken look on her face stopped him.

"I shouldn't have said that," she muttered. "I'm sorry."

"Look, Allie, I want to restore the house. It's what I do for a living. Having the Ramsdale house on my resume will boost my career and give me a lot of personal satisfaction. But I'm no thief, and if I find Otis' cache, I'll call the cops."

"Okay. I said I was sorry."

"All right, let it go." He was still irritated, though. She should have known better. But it was beginning to look as if someone was trying to scare her off by making her think the place was haunted. As for finding Otis' jewels, he had his doubts they even existed.

Chapter Four

Living in the house for a week had left Allie's nerves frazzled. Almost every morning she found something that had been moved during the night, and she heard snatches of music coming from empty rooms and strange sounds—all of which she suspected comprised a concentrated effort to drive her from the house. And she hated to answer the phone anymore. Half the time no one said anything; she heard only heavy breathing ending with a hissing sound.

Even worse, she'd stepped on an old toy truck left on the stairs yesterday and almost took a tumble. She'd managed to grab the railing, practically jerking her arm out of the socket from the way it felt, but except for a few scrapes and bruises, she had escaped injury.

Late in the afternoon she checked her supplies and made a list. A trip to the grocery store was in order. Clay was scraping loose paint from the front of the house when she left. He'd hoped to move faster on the painting, but his crew was busy finishing up a previous job, leaving him to do most of the work here. She waved at him as she drove away, thinking how much safer she felt just by his being there.

When she drove past Cora's, the woman was sitting on the front porch with a suitcase. She waved, but Cora didn't wave back, which was strange. They'd struck up a friendship of sorts, speaking when they met in the shops or if Cora happened to be in the yard when Allie walked by. Which didn't occur very often because of her father's illness.

Allie did her shopping and drove back home. Cora was

still sitting in the porch swing, although the temperature had dropped several degrees. Something didn't feel right about that. Allie turned around and drove back to park in the driveway. Cora looked in her direction when she got out of the car and walked up the front steps, but she didn't show much interest.

"You all right?"

Cora smiled, but her lips quivered. "As right as I'm going to be, I guess."

"What are you doing out here?"

"Waiting for my brother."

"What about your father?"

"He died last week. The funeral was on Friday."

Today was Monday. Allie pursed her lips. "I'm so sorry. But I don't understand why you're sitting out here in the cold."

Cora wiped her eyes. "It's so unfair. I took care of my father for six years. All that time my brother did nothing except drop in once in a while. But who did my father leave everything to? His son."

Allie sat down in the porch swing. "I'm so sorry," she said again. "What are you going to do now?"

"Oh, I'm going to live in my brother's home as an unpaid servant. I'll clean his house, see to his bratty kids, run errands for his high-maintenance wife, and I'll have absolutely no life of my own."

"But what about the house?" Allie was having trouble following all of this. "You have a home here. Why can't you stay?"

"This house and everything in it will be sold. I can't even take the furniture and other things I paid for, or what belonged to my mother. It's not right. They're legally mine, but he's stolen them from me. I have nothing except my clothes and a few personal belongings."

"I see. Wouldn't your brother let you live here if you asked him?"

"He's my half brother, and he's resented me every day of my life. He'd take a lot of enjoyment in refusing me anything I asked."

Allie shivered in the cool breeze. "Why are you waiting out here? Why not stay inside where it's warm?"

"Because he sent word to his lawyer that I should be set out on the porch with what little I was allowed to take with me and the door locked; he'd be here to pick me up at two this afternoon. He hasn't shown up yet."

Allie glanced at her watch. Five thirty. She thought for a minute. "Do you want to live with your brother?"

" 'Want to'?" Cora blazed. "I'd do anything to avoid it, but there's nothing I can do except cook and clean. I'm good at that, but I've never worked. My mother was sick and then my father, and I've had to take care of them."

Allie got to her feet, furious over what had been done to this woman. "I'm going to make you an offer. If I open a bed-and-breakfast, I'll need someone to cook and clean and help me run the place. There's a guesthouse in back. You can live there. Are you interested?"

Cora looked confused for a minute. "You're offering me a job?"

"A job and a place to live. Let your brother get by without you. You like that idea?"

"I surely do." Hope dawned on Cora's face. "Are you sure you won't regret this?"

"I'm sure." Allie reached for the suitcase. "I'm feeling in need of a friend myself right now. I don't know how all of this will work out, but we'll make it or go down together."

Cora got to her feet. "You don't what this means to me. I promise you'll never be sorry you gave me a chance. Let's go. I'm almost frozen from sitting here."

They loaded Cora's suitcase and a couple of boxes into the car, and Allie drove toward home feeling better than she had in days. If someone was trying to drive her away, they had two to fight now. And she had a hunch Cora would be a fighter. She also had a feeling they were in for a rough ride.

Allie showed Cora to an upstairs bedroom. "The guesthouse is a mess, but we'll work on it tomorrow." She got out clean sheets and helped make the bed.

"I can't believe I'm sleeping inside Miss Eliza's house." Cora spread a blanket over the sheets. "It's even more beautiful than I expected."

"Come downstairs when you're ready, and we'll talk."

Allie hurried to the kitchen to put her groceries away and started fixing a light supper.

Cora came to stand in the doorway, watching. "What can I do to help?"

"Set the table. We're just having tacos. A fix-fast meal."

"Works for me."

As they ate, Allie told Cora about her plans for the house. "I don't really know where to start."

Cora layered meat, lettuce, and tomato in a taco shell. "Well, first you have to make everything as nice as you can but homey enough to make your guests feel comfortable." She added a spoonful of shredded cheese and dribbled on sauce. "I don't remember the last time I had Mexican food. My father hated it."

"Did you always do what he wanted?"

Cora shrugged. "Most of the time, it was easier. Back to the bed-and-breakfast. When do you plan to open?"

"I haven't thought that far ahead. First I have to get the house painted and whipped into some kind of shape."

"Who's doing your work?"

"Clay Carver. We hope to start painting at the end of the week."

"I know Clay. He's good," Cora said. "I've seen a couple of houses he's worked on. Does a real professional job."

"Let's go out and look at the guesthouse and see what you think." Allie shoved leftovers into the refrigerator while Cora put the onions into a Ziploc bag and set their dishes in the sink.

Allie led the way across the yard. The door to the guesthouse swung open with a squeaking sound, and she made a mental note to oil the hinges. With a flip of the light switch, the room sprang to life.

She looked at the dingy walls and dusty floor, knowing how it must seem to Cora. "It's awful right now, but we'll clean it, paint the walls, decorate."

Cora strode through the kitchen, bedroom, bath, and back to the parlor. "Stop looking so guilty. It will be quiet, and I won't have to wait on anyone or clean up after anyone but myself. Oh, Allie, I'll scrub floors on my knees for the privilege of living here."

"Well, you won't have to do that." She could have laughed in relief. Cora, just by being there, made everything seem easier, more possible. "Let's go back to the house, and you can pick out what you want to furnish this place."

Cora stood in the middle of the room, her face flushed and eyes narrowed. "I've got a better idea. Let's go back to my father's house and take what I need from there."

"The house is locked," Allie reminded her.

"So we'll break in, unless you'd rather not," she added. "I don't want to make trouble for you. I'll take care of it myself."

"Oh, no, you don't," Allie replied. "We're in this together. I don't understand, though, why you're so fired up now, when you were so meek and accepting earlier."

"Because I'm just beginning to realize what they've done to me. I don't want the house, but I do want my mother's things and the stuff I paid for, and I have a right to them. Let's go."

Clay scanned the list of repairs he and Allie had decided on. He'd check around, get her the best deal on supplies, keep the cost as low as possible. The house had real potential for a bed-and-breakfast. The story Allie had told about the bowl of fruit bothered him. He hated to think an intruder could come and go, particularly at night when she was sleeping. Someone had a key to the place. That was the only answer. George Aiken? No, something that subtle wasn't his style. He was more the bulldozer type, running over anything that got in his way.

Maude? Maybe. But how could she have gotten hold of a key? He stared at the list again and found himself wanting to talk to Allie about a couple of items on it. He dialed her number and let it ring several times. No answer. Clay frowned at the receiver. It was night, and she didn't know very many people in

Stony Point. Where could she be? He thought about driving over to check on her, but what reason could he give? She was upset enough without his scaring her any more. Probably she'd just gone out to eat or run to the store or something. He'd talk to her tomorrow.

Allie stumbled in the dark, wishing she'd had enough sense to point out all the things wrong with this idea. She froze in trepidation as Cora picked up a rock and smashed the basement window. The tinkling of shattered glass seemed loud in the night air. They waited, listening, but no one loomed out of the darkness, yelling for them to stop.

Cora slid carefully through the broken window. "You go around to the front. That way I'm the only one breaking and entering. I'll open the door for you."

"I don't think the police will look at it that way," Allie said, but she crept around the side of the house, hoping no one was watching. She didn't know anyone in Stony Point who would put up her bail. She did have an attorney, but there was the possibility straitlaced John Bailey would dump her if she were caught in this situation. Could you be arrested for breaking into your own home? That didn't seem right, somehow.

The inside lights flashed on, and Cora opened the door and stepped back to let her enter. Allie looked around with interest.

"I cleaned, painted, and decorated—paid for it out of the small legacy I inherited from my mother. I've taken care of my father, paid the bills, and worked like a dog, and now I've been kicked out with nothing." Cora's anger warmed the room. "Let's get busy."

She strode through the house, choosing bedding, cooking utensils, and dishes. Cora chose, and Allie carried the items out to the car, packing them carefully into the trunk. A gilt-framed mirror slid between the front and back seats. Three oil paintings, a peachblow vase, a crystal basket . . . Cora had good taste.

Allie moved her car out of the way, and Cora backed a

black Ford pickup into its place. "We'll take the easy stuff first," she ordered. "That rocker, the kitchen chairs, that small chest in my bedroom."

She indicated a long, low bookcase in the room that had been hers. "I paid for that, and I'm taking it with me."

They almost had the pickup loaded when two men walked up the short driveway. The tallest one spoke. "What you doing, Cora?"

She whirled to meet them, and Allie's hand went to her throat. What would happen now? She'd known this wouldn't work.

Cora faced them, head high. "I'm moving into the guesthouse at Miss Eliza's. I need furniture."

"Blakely know about that?"

Cora looked whipped again. As if she knew she wouldn't get away from her brother after all. "No," she whispered. "I don't guess he does, Deke."

"I see," Deke said. "Well, I never felt right about you going to live with him and that wife of his. You need any help?"

Cora's shoulders sagged. "You'll help me?"

"Sure will," he replied. "Everyone on this block knows how hard you worked and the way you took care of your dad. Not that he ever appreciated it. Him and that brother of yours are cut out of the same bolt of cloth. Now, what do you need?"

Cora pointed out the stove and the refrigerator. Allie hastened to empty the fridge so they could move it. They took one load to the guesthouse and came back for the couch and chairs, a bed and dresser, and the kitchen table.

Allie paused in front of the entertainment center. "You'll need a television."

"That she will," Bill, the shorter man, said. "Computer too."

"The computer?" Longing flickered in Cora's expression. "I bought it, but do you think I should?"

"Why not?" Deke laughed. "Too late to start worrying about it now."

"I guess so." Cora unhooked the cables, and Bill carried the tower and monitor outside while Allie followed with the printer.

Deke stopped in the doorway of one bedroom, and Cora whirled on him. "I want nothing from that room."

He nodded and closed the door again. From Cora's expression, Allie supposed it was her father's room. No matter what he had intended, that sick old man had destroyed whatever love his daughter had held for him.

Cora added an armload of photo albums to the pile of selected items and looked around the room. "I guess that's it. I suppose I ought to nail something over the window I broke to get in."

"Me and Deke'll take care of that," Bill said. "Don't worry about it."

Cora nodded. "Thanks. I'll lock up."

The men left, and Allie heard them drive away. Cora looked around the parlor, tears welling in her eyes. "I don't suppose I'll ever come back again. I've lived here all my life, and now I realize it was more of a prison than a home."

"You're free to do what you want now," Allie said.

Cora's shoulders stiffened. "And the first thing I'm going to do is see a lawyer and fight that will."

Back at the Ramsdale mansion, they unloaded everything and put it into the guesthouse. Bill and Deke waited while Allie locked the door. Cora looked at her watch. "It's almost midnight, and I'm worn out."

Deke shoved his hands inside his jacket pockets. "One thing I've always wanted was to see inside Miss Eliza's house, but she wasn't much for company. Always admired it, though."

"When we get things settled a bit, we'll have you and your wives to dinner," Allie promised.

Bill turned to look at the house. "That sounds like a winner. It used to be one of the prettiest homes in town."

"It's going to be pretty again," Allie said. "We're starting to paint next week."

They said good-bye to the two men and walked back to the house. The dishes from their impromptu meal were still stacked in the sink.

"We're too tired and dirty to mess with them," Allie said.

"You take the bathroom first. Tomorrow we'll tackle the guesthouse. You'll soon have your own space with your own things around you."

Cora hesitated at the top of the stairs. "Allie, I didn't steal anything tonight. I didn't take one thing that wasn't legally mine."

"I know. Don't worry about it. But tomorrow you go see John Bailey and tell him everything."

"I will, I promise." Cora groaned. "I'm so tired, I could drop down right here and go to sleep."

"Well, don't. I can assure you, that's a good bed in your room. You'll sleep well."

As soon as she heard Cora leave the bathroom, Allie hurried to take her bath. Later she turned out the light in her bedroom and stood by the window for a moment, watching the moon slide silently through silvered drifts of clouds.

A movement below claimed her attention. A slight figure dressed in white slid away from the house to merge with the shadows of the lilac bush. Allie strained to see, but whatever had been there was gone now. It had looked like a woman. She shivered and rubbed her arms, feeling cold, although the room was warm enough. Had that ghostly figure been in the house tonight? What would she find when she went downstairs in the morning?

Chapter Five

Allie woke with a sense of dread. What would she find moved around today? She hadn't told Cora about the strange happenings—she was afraid to. She needed Cora. Just having her in the house made it less lonely. True, she would be moving to the guesthouse as soon as it was livable, but she'd still be on the property.

As she watched from the tower room, the skiff of clouds in the eastern sky changed from the soft gray of a dove's breast to a muted peach rimmed with pure gold. The sun was about to begin its ponderous daylong march across the sky. Birds in the old oak tree outside her window stirred and twittered, roused by the golden rays lancing through the rustling leaves. Morning had arrived. She loved sunrises. Sunsets might be more spectacular, but they held sadness. Another day done. Sunrises were a new beginning. A new day filled with promise. She hurriedly selected fresh clothing: shabby jeans, overly long T-shirt, and sneakers. Today, deep cleaning and putting the small guest cottage into order was number one on her to-do list. She wanted Cora to be happy, and having her own apartment would help.

The fragrance of fresh-brewed coffee wafted up to meet her as she made her way downstairs, and the sound of voices drew her like a magnet. Clay sat at the table, wolfing down pancakes and Canadian bacon. Allie stopped in the doorway, eyebrows raised. She was paying him a hefty sum to paint the house, and now she was feeding him too? That wasn't in the contract.

He looked up and saw her—saw what she was thinking too, because he flushed. "This isn't an everyday thing."

"Oh?" Her tone of voice said she certainly hoped not.

Cora turned from the stove, looking refreshed. "I'm feeding him because he's going to help with the guesthouse. Isn't that great?"

"Oh." Allie felt that she had been reprimanded. "Well . . . that's nice of him."

A long peal from the doorbell gave her an opportunity to back off. It *was* nice of Clay to offer to help, and, after all, she was paying him by the job, not the hour, so his helping Cora wouldn't cost her anything except what he ate. It wasn't that she begrudged the money, but that seventy-five thousand wouldn't last long, and there remained a lot of work to be done before she could open her business.

Another drawn-out peal sent her scurrying to answer. Bill and Deke stood on the porch, wearing sheepish expressions. She blinked, wondering why they were there.

Deke shuffled his feet. "Uh . . . me and Bill, we got to thinking."

"Yes?" She'd help him out if she could, but she had no idea where this was going.

"We was wondering maybe if we could do something to make that place out back more homey-like for Cora."

"See, people in our neighborhood respect her," Bill added. "She's a nice lady."

Allie hesitated, not sure what to say. She'd designated the guesthouse for Cora. It was up to Cora to decide what she wanted.

Deke misinterpreted her hesitation. "We wouldn't want no pay for helping."

"That's right," Bill said earnestly. "We just want to lend a hand."

Allie opened the door wider. "You'll have to talk to Cora. She's making the decisions concerning the guesthouse."

They followed her to the kitchen, where Clay nursed a cup of coffee. From his satisfied expression, she guessed he'd tanked up on pancakes and bacon. Cora, still at the stove, looked puzzled, then apprehensive.

Allie hurried to reassure her. "Deke and Bill want to help make the guesthouse more livable."

To her consternation, tears filled Cora's eyes, and she turned to face the window.

Deke looked uncomfortable. "We didn't mean to upset you none."

"No, see, we was just wanting to help," Bill chimed in.

Cora turned around to look at them, tears running down her cheeks. "It's not that. I just can't remember when anyone ever did something for me simply because they wanted to."

Allie stepped into the breach. "Coffee, anyone?" she babbled, giving her friend a chance to compose herself.

Bill and Deke pulled out chairs, and Allie brought cups filled to the brim. "Sugar, creamer?"

Cora, under control now, smiled brightly. "And there's pancakes."

"Pancakes?" Bill sat up straighter.

"With maple syrup," Clay said. "Those flapjacks are feather-light and taste like manna from heaven."

Deke pursed his lips, eyes alight with anticipation. "Well, if it ain't too much trouble, I might be persuaded to partake."

"No trouble at all," Cora assured him. "Not after what you've done for me."

Even Allie couldn't begrudge them the food, although she did some hasty mental arithmetic refiguring her budget.

After half an hour passed while they filled up on pancakes and Canadian bacon and drank a full pot of coffee, Allie gathered cleaning supplies and led the way out to the guest-house. It was worth a few pancakes to have three husky men along to do the lifting. They'd also come in really handy if whoever was playing tricks on her showed up.

Clay took the mop, broom, and pail full of cleaning supplies from Allie and followed her out to the guesthouse. With Bill and Deke to help, he could get back to scraping. He wanted to start painting tomorrow. Allie strode out in front, leading the way, ponytail bouncing. Even wearing ragged jeans and that ratty T-shirt, she looked good. She was a lot more relaxed today too. Maybe having Cora with her helped. That big old house was probably lonesome at night. Not that she'd ever admit she was scared or needed anyone. She opened the door to the guesthouse, and they all trooped in. Clay stared in amazement at the furniture now filling what had been an empty room the last time he'd looked.

"Where'd all this stuff come from?"

Cora and Allie exchanged looks. Deke stared out the window while Bill developed a strong interest in a big black water bug crawling across the floor.

A prickle of apprehension inched up Clay's spine. What was going on here? He caught Allie's eyes, noticing the defiance lingering in their depths.

"What have you done?"

"Nothing." The angle of her chin said she wasn't about to give him any information. He'd bet his shirt that, whatever had happened, she was up to her pretty neck in it.

He shifted his attention to Cora. "You feel like talking?"

She glanced away, then looked back at him. "I might as well tell you. It won't be a secret for long anyway."

That sounded ominous. "What won't?"

"We broke into my father's house last night and took out the furniture I needed for this place."

He gasped at the sheer audacity of it. "You broke . . . broke . . ." Words failed him.

Cora nodded.

"Broke into Blakely's house and took furniture?" Clay recovered his voice. "Are you crazy?"

Cora looked belligerent. "I only took what was rightfully mine."

He considered that, allowing she was probably telling the truth. Still . . . "Look, we both know your brother is the meanest, stingiest, most cantankerous jerk to come down the pike."

She nodded. "That he is."

"You talked to an attorney about this?"

"We're going to," Allie said, "We just haven't gotten around to it yet."

"Well, you can get around to it right now. Cora, you get yourself back to the house and call that attorney."

"Sure, Clay, I'll do that." Cora edged past Deke on her way toward the door. "But I'm going to contest that will too."

"All the more reason to talk to an attorney." Clay fixed Allie with a jaundiced eye. This woman was going to be trouble; he could feel it in his bones.

Bill and Deke were piling furniture into the middle of the parlor, preparing to cover it with a sheet of plastic. Cora had decided to paint all the walls white, and the two men had volunteered to do the work. Since they didn't need her, Allie decided to go back to the house and do some cleaning there while Cora was at John Bailey's office.

She had just gotten to the top of the stairs when the phone rang, meaning she had to clamber back down the steps to catch it before it stopped. She grabbed it on the fourth ring, out of breath from hurrying.

A man's voice, abrupt and angry, exploded in her ear. "Cora there?"

Allie held the receiver away from her, staring at it. "I beg your pardon?"

"Cora Witner. She there?"

"Not at the moment."

"Where is she, then? Down at my house, stealing me blind?"

"Who is this?" Although by now Allie had a fairly good idea who was ranting over her phone line.

"This is Blakely Witner, her brother. I need to talk to her. Pronto."

"Like I said, she isn't here. If you'll leave your number . . ."

"Hiding out, is she? Good idea. Breaking and entering and stealing. That's against the law. My old dad would be rolling over in his grave if he knew how she'd turned out. Barely let his body get cold before she started swiping things from him."

Allie pressed her lips shut in an effort to keep from telling the man what she thought of his "old dad" and of him too. Just this brief encounter was enough to make her glad Cora hadn't gone to live with the man.

"You there?" Blakely demanded.

"I'm here."

"Good. Don't you go hanging up on me before I'm through. Got a message for my baby sister." The words *baby sister* held a world of venom.

"Why didn't you come to pick her up?" Allie asked.

The question seemed to take him by surprise. "Eh?"

"You were supposed to be there by two. I brought her home with me at five thirty, and you still hadn't come by seven. Where were you?"

"Now see here!" he blustered. "I was detained."

"It was cold, and you'd had her locked out. How do you think that would look in court?"

"In court!" He sounded alarmed. "Now, who said anything about court?"

"You were talking about the law."

"Well, yes. But that was just a figure of speech. Who are you anyway?"

"Allison McGregor. I own the Ramsdale house. Are you in Stony Point?"

"Well, no, not right at the moment." He sounded less sure of himself.

"Did you ever come to get her? You were supposed to pick her up the day before yesterday. It's now two days later, and you haven't shown up yet? That's inhumane."

"Now, just listen a minute, will you? It wasn't as bad as Cora let on. I'd talked to the attorney handling things for me. He was supposed to let her back inside until I could get there."

"That's the same lawyer who locked her out in the first place, right?"

"That's neither here nor there. Main thing is, I want her to take back everything she hauled out of that house, and I want it back by nightfall."

"Cora only took what belonged to her. If you didn't come to Stony Point, how do you know so much about what happened?"

"I have my sources." He sounded smug.

Allie's flimsy grip on her temper gave way completely. "Well, 'source' this. Cora has witnesses to what you did. Locked out of her own house with only her clothes. Your sister is well thought of here, and people are upset over the sorry way she's been treated."

He laughed. "But they can't do anything about it, now, can they?"

"You just might be surprised. I'll tell Cora you called. She can call back if she wants to talk to you." She slammed down the receiver, seething at the rude arrogance of this man. No wonder Clay had such a bad opinion of Blakely Witner. Cora would never have to live with that full-fledged, gold-plated jerk, if she, Allie McGregor, had anything to say about it.

Clay stepped back and looked up at the Ramsdale house. They'd finished scraping and were in the processing of applying primer. He couldn't wait to put on the first coat of gray paint. He knew just how it would look. This beautiful old house would be restored in all its former glory, and he'd have a part in it. Life was good.

His cell phone rang, and he reached absently for it. "Hello?"

"Hello, darling," Gilda cooed. "How's everything at the old homestead?"

"Fine." He didn't want Gilda intruding on his space right now.

"I have important information for you."

"Oh, yeah? What?"

"You'll have to do better than that. Aren't you glad to hear from me?"

He forced himself to be calm. "Of course I am. It's just that I'm rather busy right now."

"Little Miss McGregor keeping you occupied, no doubt?"

"No, we're putting on primer."

"That might be a waste of time, darling."

Was it his imagination, or was there a tinge of satisfaction in the words, a sarcastic emphasis on the word *darling*? The impact of what she had just said hit him. "What are you talking about?"

"George Aiken filed a lawsuit today, claiming his wife has a stronger right to the Ramsdale house, since she's Otis' great-niece."

Clay felt like he'd been punched in the stomach. "He can't do that."

"He already has."

There was more, but Clay quit listening. He ended the call and then realized he'd cut Gilda off in midsentence. He'd pay for that. A lawsuit? But there was a will. Drawn by John Bailey. Surely it would stand up in court.

Allie needed to know this, and she would be crushed. He realized that that mattered to him. He glanced up once more at the graceful old house, catching sight of a shadowy form behind the sheer curtains Allie had hung in the tower room. She was probably up there right now, just enjoying her special place. He waved, but apparently she didn't see him.

He dreaded what he had to tell her. She would be shattered. He knew how badly she wanted this house and the bed-and-breakfast she had planned. And what about him? He wanted to finish working on the place. Clay strode toward the front door, planning on calling Allie down to hear the bad news. Instead, when he opened the door, he found her in the foyer, dusting the statue of Mercury. He jerked to a stop, looking up the stairs. How did she get down there so fast?

"Cora back yet?" Maybe that was the answer. Must not have been Allie standing at the window.

Allie shook her head. "No. I don't know if that's a good sign or not. I'm getting ready to start lunch. Deke and Bill will be eating here. Do you want to join us?"

He was surprised at how much he wanted to, but it wouldn't be a good idea. "No, I'll eat with my crew."

"Oh, of course." She blushed, and he decided she sure looked cute when she got flustered. He hated to tell her the news, but she'd find it out anyway, and she needed to be prepared.

"Listen, Allie. Gilda Latimer just called. George Aiken has filed a suit against you, claiming this house belongs to his wife."

She paled, and he reached out to steady her. "That's absurd. Aunt Eliza left this house to me."

"I know that, and it'll work out—don't worry." He'd do enough worrying for both of them. George Aiken wasn't used to being blocked from getting his own way. He would cause as much trouble as possible, trying to force Allie out of the Ramsdale house. Something else bothered him. Who had been upstairs in the tower room?

Allie looked around the foyer at the beautiful paneling, the parquet floor. She loved this house, but she didn't have the money to fight a lawsuit. Even if she won, there wouldn't be anything left over to restore the place or start the business she wanted so much. She had made her plans, sure everything would work out all right; now there was a chance she would lose it all. Could she give up the house, now that she had experienced what it could be like living here? It would tear her apart. She absently ran the dust cloth over the statue of Mercury, thinking she wouldn't say anything to Cora just yet. Time enough for that when she found out where she stood.

Cora got home an hour later, loaded with two large paper bags of groceries. "I thought I'd better stock up again if we're going to be feeding Deke and Bill. They both make good hands at the table."

Allie followed her to the kitchen. "You had a phone call."

Cora stopped in the act of removing cans of vegetables from one of the paper sacks. "Blakely?"

"Uh-huh."

"Was he mad?"

"Oh, high octane."

Cora shrugged. "Too bad. He's going to be sorry if he messes with me."

"What did Mr. Bailey say?"

"Scolded me for breaking in. Said he didn't blame me, and then he started working on a bill for wages due me for taking care of my father. Comes to a nice round sum. I don't think Blakely will have time to worry about a few pieces of furniture. My big brother is going to have a fight on his hands."

Allie climbed the stairs, feeling worn down. She'd sent Cora up to bed earlier while she sorted through the papers crammed into Aunt Eliza's desk. Not that she'd found anything important, but it had to be done. Now she was ready for bed.

A foul odor hit her nostrils before she pushed open the bedroom door. She flipped the switch and paused, aghast. A dead rabbit lay in the center of her bed. Plastic flowers, faded and dirty, were arranged around the animal's body, like a funeral offering. Allie stepped back and closed the door, taking a deep breath. How could someone have smuggled this into the house without being caught?

She crept back downstairs for a couple of trash bags. It was important to get that mess out of the house before Cora saw it. Allie wiped the ready tears from her eyes. She was tired and discouraged, not sure what to do anymore. Someone was determined to drive her from this house. How far were they willing to go, and what would happen next?

Chapter Six

Allie smiled at Cora across the breakfast table. "Well, this is the big day. Are you ready?"

"As ready as I'll ever be. Do you realize I've never lived alone?"

"It will be different, but if you get lonely, your old room will still be here."

"Until we fill up with lodgers." Cora lifted her coffee cup. "To our business enterprise, the Ramsdale House Bed-and-Breakfast."

They clinked their cups together. "Hear, hear." Allie swallowed a mouthful of coffee wrong and ended up in a coughing fit.

Cora pounded her on the back. "Are you all right?"

"I will be if you quit beating on me," Allie gasped. "Leave off, will you?"

"I was trying to help."

"I appreciate it, I think."

"Maybe I was a little too enthusiastic," Cora admitted, "but you sounded like you were dying."

"Felt like it for a minute too. Are we ready?"

"I guess so."

Allie led the way to the guesthouse, where Cora was to take up residence that day. "You know, I meant what I said. If you're nervous staying here by yourself, you can move into a room at the main house, and we'll rent out the cottage. It's up to you."

"No, I like the idea of being on my own. I can do exactly as

I please, and for the first time in my life I'm not responsible for anyone except myself."

Allie handed her the key. "Okay, in you go."

Cora unlocked the door and stepped inside, coming to an abrupt stop. A large bouquet of cut flowers in shades of blue, white, and pink sat on the coffee table. A banner stretched across the living room wall behind the couch read, *Welcome home.*

"Oh, my." Cora had tears in her eyes. "You did this?"

Allie nodded. "I hope you'll be very happy here."

"Oh, I know I will be. Allie, how can I ever thank you?"

"By being my friend. I'm just beginning to realize how badly I needed one, and how well you fill that need."

"You fill a need for me too. It was a good day when we met."

"It was at that. Now I'm going to leave you alone for a while to get settled in. I know you still have things to do. Come over to the main house when you're ready, and we'll do some planning. I'd like to go over the stuff in the attic and see what we can use. Maybe sell the rest."

Cora looked around the room. "This is going to take some getting used to, but I think I'm going to love it."

"I hope so. If not, you can have your pick of rooms in the house."

Cora hesitated. "I know I'm being silly, but I'm not all that comfortable in the house. Something seems a little off-kilter."

Allie hesitated. How to ask this without making Cora even more uncomfortable? She decided there wasn't any way to beat around the bush. "Have you seen or heard anything?"

Cora got a cautious expression. "Maybe."

"I see. We seem to have a few things to talk about. See you later." Allie walked back to the house, wondering what had put that look onto Cora's face. She'd been living in the house for a week now, plenty of time to notice some of the strange things that kept happening. Just yesterday Allie had found the living room mantel clock in the office, sitting right in the middle of her desk. She'd moved it back to the mantel and said nothing, not wanting to make a big deal out of it. Evidently Cora had had her own experiences. It would be interesting putting them together.

The phone rang just as she entered the kitchen from the back door. She hurried through to the living room to answer. As soon as she got around to it, they were putting in more lines. One in her bedroom, the kitchen, the office—at least that many.

"Hello?"

"Who is this?"

"Whom were you calling?"

"Allie McGregor."

"Speaking."

"You don't know me, but I'm a friend. You are in very grave danger. You must move out of that house before something tragic happens. The house isn't for you."

The line went dead.

A shiver of fear prickled the hairs on Allie's arms. This constant harassment was getting to her. Who was so determined to drive her out of this house, and why?

Cora entered the kitchen, clutching a spiral notebook. "You ready to get started?"

"I guess so. What are we doing?"

"We're making a list of things we *want* to do, and then we're going to decide what we *can* do, and then we're going to *do* it."

"Sounds like a plan." Allie poured coffee and got her own notepad. "Where do we start?"

"Well, I've been thinking about this. First of all, we need queen-size beds."

"We have beds. Why do we need to buy new ones?" Allie cringed as she thought of how her legacy was dribbling away to nothing. "I can't afford new beds."

"You can't afford not to have them. I've done something you may not like, and if so, I'll apologize. I asked Lita Newcome to stop by and look at the existing bedroom furniture and see what kind of price she'd give you."

"Who's she?"

"Lita owns that antique shop downtown. She'll make you a good deal. Now, we'll need matching bed linen, with extra blankets and sheets stored in the rooms."

"Stored in what? I'm not made of money."

"I figure we can pick up some of those wicker cabinets pretty cheap. A comfortable chair in each room, two pillows for each guest. A reading lamp and an alarm clock in every room."

Allie tapped her pen against the notepad. "Anything else?"

"Yes." Cora grinned. "I thought we could use some of those flat-topped trunks in the attic for a table at the foot of the bed, and we need another table where we can put a basket of goodies, business cards, stationery, candy, maybe fruit."

"Good idea," Allie approved. "You've come up with some great suggestions. When can this Lita person come by?"

"This afternoon. That all right with you?"

"I guess so. Now, what are we going to do about the foyer? That's the first thing people will see."

"Let's look."

They stood in the foyer, looking around at the paneled walls. "Actually, there's not much we can do," Allie admitted. "We don't dare touch the paneling or the floor—Clay would have a conniption fit."

"White walls above the paneling until we can afford the right kind of wallpaper?" Cora asked. "We don't want to put curtains over those frosted-glass entry doors. Clean the chandelier and have the love seat and chairs upholstered, and that's about it."

"Get rid of that gloomy picture of Washington crossing the Delaware," Allie suggested. "We can probably find a suitable replacement in the attic."

They moved into the living room.

"Probably." Cora sounded distracted. "Where did you put the Dresden shepherdess?"

Allie stared at her, bewildered. "The who?"

"That little figurine of a girl herding sheep. It stood right there next to the clock on the mantel."

Allie felt her expression stiffen.

Cora narrowed her eyes. "You do know what I'm talking about?"

"I know the shepherdess. I don't know where she is."

"Would you like to explain that?"

"I don't have an explanation."

"You're saying things are being moved, and you don't know who is doing it?"

"I guess so." She watched Cora for some sign of fear. Something to say she wasn't going to go into business in a house where things moved by themselves.

Cora sat down in one of the chairs. "I hoped I was wrong and you'd been moving things, but I didn't see how you could be. I tried to watch, but I never saw anything."

"You've had things moved too?"

Cora nodded. "Things in my bedroom were moved to another room. I like to read in my bath. A book I left in the bathroom turned up in the office. I thought you might have picked it up, gotten interested, and carried it downstairs."

Allie shook her head. "Not me. I don't know anything about it."

"You've had some strange experiences too, haven't you? Because you asked me earlier if I'd seen or heard anything. What have you seen? And I want straight answers."

Allie took a deep breath. "Are you going to leave?"

Cora shook her head in exasperation. "Where would I go? I'm just trying to find out what we're up against."

"You're not leaving." Allie sagged in relief. She didn't have to worry about that at any rate. "Okay, give me a minute to decide where to start."

"Start at the beginning. That way you don't have to keep backing and filling. I want the truth, and I want it all. Don't hold anything back."

"All right. That big milk-glass bowl on the kitchen table was the first thing to be moved, or that I noticed anyway."

"I see. When was that?"

"Right after I came here. Clay was here that day with paint samples. I think it was the day I first met you."

"Clay wouldn't do anything like that."

"I don't think he would either." But then, she didn't know him all that well. How did she know what he would do? She realized she didn't want it to be Clay. Refused to believe it could be him. And it didn't have a thing to do with the way she kept watching for a glimpse of him, or the way he made her feel safe and protected.

"Go on, then what?"

Allie told her about the music and about the woman dressed in white she'd seen leaving the house.

Cora pounced on that. "You think she'd been inside?"

"I don't know. I'd had all the locks changed by then, and I don't see how she could have gotten in."

"You're not operating on the theory that this is some supernatural stuff, are you?"

"Of course not." Allie shook her head in denial. "I don't believe in ghosts."

"Me neither," Cora said, her expression glum. "Might be easier if we did. Get the local pastor or priest, or someone like Maude Wheeler, to come chase them out. But I don't believe in that junk, which means we have a real problem."

"You don't think a resident ghost would be a problem?" Allie grinned. "I'm impressed."

"Oh, we could just ignore a ghost. Call it window dressing, but since neither of us believes in ghosts and goblins, we're faced with the fact that someone is trying to drive us out of the house."

"You just figured that out?" Allie asked. "George Aiken is suing me, Maude and Mary want to buy me out, and who knows how many others want in? And that reminds me." She told Cora about the phone call.

" 'This house is not for you'? That's what he said?"

"Word for word."

"Hmm. Be interesting to know who he did think it was for. You reckon Maude got a member of her group to make that call?"

"Or George, or maybe Blakely getting his own back. I was sort of rough on him when he called."

"Good. I plan to be rough on him myself if he ever calls again."

Allie sighed. "What do we do now?"

"We don't do anything. If this person wanted to hurt us, he'd already have done so, but I want you to move over to the guesthouse until we figure out what is going on."

"No. I'm staying right here, and you are not going to move back into this house to take care of me either. We're not going to live in fear. I will not allow this person to run me off or make me change my way of living. When we find out who is responsible, we'll take it from there."

"Way to go," Cora said admiringly, with only a touch of sarcasm. "Brave woman."

"Hardly. I can't afford to run. This house is all I have. I can't lose it because I didn't have enough backbone to fight."

Although what she would do if she met their mysterious intruder was anyone's guess. She had to put up a strong front, though. She was the owner here. "We're going to catch them."

"How?"

"Beats me," Allie said. "But we're gonna do it."

Clay walked into the kitchen, where Allie and Cora were poring over their notes. "I've got the estimate on the sound-proofing for the bedrooms. A guy I know is willing to give us a good price."

Allie smiled inwardly at his use of the word *us*. Sounded natural too, as if he really thought that way. She knew he meant they were a team, working together to restore the house, and she also knew how much being able to do the restoration meant to him. She'd told him that John Bailey had reassured her that the will couldn't be broken. The house was hers. She hoped the lawyer was right. Otherwise, she was going to owe for the repairs on this place with no way to pay for them.

Maybe she could keep the money Aunt Eliza had left her, if worse came to worst and she lost the house.

After Howard, she had planned to be through with men, but, like most of her plans, it didn't seem to be working out that way. She was becoming more aware of Clay all the time.

She tried to concentrate on the sheaf of figures instead of the faint whiff of his aftershave. "Well, maybe we can swing that. Cora has come up with an idea of selling the antiques we don't plan to use in the bed-and-breakfast. She thinks we need queen-sized beds."

"Good idea. And, of course, you're going to need another bathroom on the second floor and one on the third."

Allie sighed at the thought of so much money going out of her pocket. There wouldn't be a lot left over for operating expenses.

Cora left to answer the phone. She was just gone a minute before returning. "It's for you, Allie."

She entered the parlor, absently thinking of where to put the new bathroom. The voice on the phone brought her up short.

"Allie? I haven't heard from you since your childish display of temper. I hope you've got the rebellion out of your system and are ready to come home. Your parents are having as much trouble as I am in understanding why you're acting like this."

"Howard?"

"You recognized my voice. I was afraid, as long as you've been gone, you wouldn't."

Oh, she recognized it all right. Her temper heat index was climbing higher than the noonday sun. "I thought I made it clear that I wasn't coming back."

"I'm willing to overlook that. Your father tells me you've inherited one of the large homes in Stony Point."

"Yes, I have." And what did that have to do with this call?

"I've decided to make a run for state representative. With you by my side and a home in Stony Point to use for entertaining, we'd be a winning combination."

"Forget it, Howard. I'm not interested in being the little

political wife. Right now I'm planning on opening a bed-and-breakfast."

"You always did think small, Allie."

"Right. Like when I once thought you were the man for me. I'm aiming higher now. Good-bye, Howard. Don't call again."

She hung up the receiver and took a couple of deep breaths, trying to calm down before going back to the kitchen to face Clay and Cora. Her eyes focused on the gold-framed mirror over the fireplace. The words, written in what looked like lipstick, glowed in bright burgundy. *We don't want you here. Get out.*

Allie rushed back to the kitchen. "Clay! The mirror!"

He was on his feet in a second. "What's wrong? What happened?"

"In there." She gestured toward the parlor, and he pushed past her, followed by Cora. Allie trailed behind them, reluctant to face that ugly message.

Clay looked at her, his expression bewildered. She pointed up at the mirror and watched his shocked reaction. Cora gasped, the sound loud in the silence, and the two of them stood as if rooted to the spot, reading the corrosive words, while Allie watched their expressions. Unless they were accomplished actors, they were truly surprised.

"Who wrote that?" Clay demanded.

Allie shook her head. "I don't know. I hung up the phone and glanced up at the mirror, and there it was."

Cora held out her hands beseechingly. "I didn't see it, Allie. I swear I didn't. I would not have sent you in there to face something like that. I'd have cleaned it off, like . . ." She slid to a halt, looking as if she wished she'd said nothing

"Like what, Cora?" Clay asked. "Like always? You've seen messages like these before?"

Cora nodded. "In the bathroom before I moved out. And on the mirrors in a couple of bedrooms."

Clay frowned. "What's going on here?"

"Nothing is—" Allie began.

Cora cut in, interrupting her. "Yes, something *is* going on. There's been a systematic attempt to scare Allie into leaving. They're getting bolder all the time, and we need to do something about it before it gets out of hand."

"What do you suggest we do?" Allie demanded. She waved a hand in the general direction of the fireplace and the mirror. "Either one of us could have done that."

Cora stood a little straighter. "You think I did it?"

"No, I don't, but the police would be bound to consider it."

"Why would we do that?"

"Who knows? Maybe we wanted publicity. After all, we're going to open a bed-and-breakfast one of these days. Or that's the plan, anyway."

"And pretending someone is trying to drive us out or we have a ghost would help us there?" Cora was plainly skeptical.

"The important thing is, who can come and go undetected? I thought you had the locks changed," Clay said.

"I did," Allie said defensively. "You were here the day they were being changed."

"Who has keys?"

"You, Cora, and me."

"That's it?"

"Right. Just the three of us."

"There must be a door someplace we've missed," Clay mused aloud. "But we've been all around the place scraping and painting. Someone would have noticed it."

"You're not staying here by yourself at night anymore," Cora said. "There's plenty of room at the guesthouse."

"No. I'm not going to be run off from my own home." Allie glowered at them. "Whoever is doing this is planning to push me out, but I'm staying."

Even as she said the words, she felt a ripple of fear at the idea of being alone in the house at night. The thought of an unknown someone creeping through the rooms while she slept filled her with dread. She wanted to give in, but her pride wouldn't let her. This was her fight, and she couldn't run away.

*   *   *

The night passed without incident, and when Allie looked through the rooms in the morning, nothing seemed out of place. She suspected this was deliberate. A war of nerves keeping her off balance, so she'd never know when her unknown enemy would strike again.

Sunday morning Allie and Cora drove downtown to the Court Street House of Grace, Cora's church. The building was comfortably full, but Allie didn't see anyone she knew. She noticed a dark-haired man smiling at Cora. When Cora smiled back, Allie's antenna went up. Who was this? She'd thought Cora hadn't had time for male friendships, but the way these two looked at each other said they weren't your ordinary casual acquaintances. Afterward she lingered out front, smiling and chatting with a few people who stopped to visit. Cora and the man stood a little way off, talking and laughing.

An older woman, white hair glistening in the sun, faded blue eyes twinkling with life, stopped in front of her. "You're Eliza's great-niece. Have I got that right?"

"Yes, I am. Allie McGregor."

"Anna Milcrest. Eliza and I were good friends. Stop in and see me someday."

"I'd love to do that. Where do you live?"

"Next street over from the Ramsdales, Second Empire to her Queen Anne, cream with gold shutters. You can't miss it. Just drop in whenever you have the time. I'm always home, and I'd like to talk to you about Eliza. You probably don't know much about her."

"I don't know anything about her," Allie said. "I'd really like to talk to you. How about tomorrow afternoon around two?"

"That would be just fine." A young man joined them and took Anna's elbow. She grinned up at him. "This is my grandson. He's supposed to be watching me so I don't fall, but I slipped away from him."

"You sure did. If you're not careful, you're going to get me into trouble." He smiled at Allie. "She pretty well does what she wants."

"At my age, I've earned that right." Anna tapped Allie on the arm. "Tomorrow. I'll be looking forward to it."

She strolled away, leaning on the young man's arm.

Cora approached. "I saw you talking to Anna Milcrest. What did she have on her mind?"

"She really didn't say much, just that she wanted to talk to me about Aunt Eliza."

"Well, if anyone could tell you about her, Anna can. She knows everyone who is anyone in this town. Of course, she doesn't get out much anymore, so her reminiscences will be mostly from the distant past, but I guess that's what you're interested in."

The crowd had thinned out, and they got into the car and drove home. "So who was the guy?" Allie asked.

"What guy?"

"Don't play coy with me. That good-looking man who kept me waiting for fifteen minutes while he talked to you."

"It wasn't fifteen minutes. You're exaggerating. More like ten."

"Ten, fifteen, it doesn't matter. Come on, give. Who is he?"

"His name is Roger Axelrod. I went to school with him."

"I see."

"No, you don't see," Cora said. "Don't try to make anything out of this. He's someone I used to know, but I haven't seen him for years. His wife died last summer, and he moved back to Stony Point."

"No past romance?" Allie persisted.

"Like I had a chance to have a romance." Cora sounded bitter. "He did ask me out a couple of times when we were younger, but my father refused to let me go."

Probably afraid he'd lose his unpaid servant, Allie thought unkindly. "Well, there's no reason you can't be friends. Look, Cora, you're on your own now. You can do whatever you want, and no one can stop you. What would be wrong with you and Roger spending time together? You have a lot of catching up to do."

"Too much to ever catch up, on my part," Cora said, turning

her head to look out the window. Her voice was muffled. "I'm just beginning to realize how much of life I've missed out on."

"You don't have to continue missing out on it. Life is out there waiting for you. Embrace it." *Good advice.* Now, if she could just follow it herself. Maybe she was, to some extent, by opening the Ramsdale House Bed-and-Breakfast. At least it was different from anything she'd ever done.

Allie pulled into the driveway and stopped, staring in disbelief at the two women seated in wicker chairs on the front porch. Maude Wheeler and Mary Olson. What were they doing there?

"Uh-oh. Here comes trouble," Cora muttered. "Good thing we locked the house when we left."

They got out of the car and approached the steps. Maude watched them with a haughty expression on her face. "It's about time you got home. I'm not used to being kept waiting."

"I don't remember making an appointment with you." Allie made no effort to unlock the door. This woman had thrown her out of the bookshop the last time they'd met, and she hadn't forgotten it. "What do you want?"

Maude got to her feet. "I came to demand that the work you're doing come to an immediate halt. The house belongs to me on a level you cannot begin to comprehend. You must turn it over to me. I will pay you a reasonable price for it, of course."

Allie fought a rising anger. "For the last time, the house is not for sale. What's with you people? Can't you understand plain English?"

Maude ignored Allie's outburst. "I would suggest you leave as soon as possible. Otherwise I will not be responsible for what vengeance the spirits will wreak on you and the others who defile my house by their presence."

Before Allie could answer, Mary turned on Maude, her face flushed with anger. "I do wish you'd stop calling it *your* house. It isn't, you know."

Maude drew back as if a pet mouse had roared. "You know very well this house was mine in another life. In fact, I had it built, which is how I know the original color, and what this woman has chosen is all wrong."

Mary looked stubborn. "I *don't* know it belonged to you. I have more right to it than you do."

Maude bristled. "You know very well, Mary, the spirits have said it belongs to me. Are you going to argue with the spirits?"

"I wouldn't put it past you to make that up just so you can weasel the house away from me."

Maude's face was almost purple with rage. She raised a forefinger, stabbing in Mary's direction. "You dare question me? Have you no fear?"

Before Mary could answer, Cora cut in. "I've had enough of this. The house belongs to Allie. Eliza left it to her. You have no business here, stirring up trouble. Go on, leave. I'm hungry, and I'm not standing around out here any longer."

Maude swung around to face her. "It's not for you to tell us what to do," she began, but Allie interrupted.

"If you are not off this porch in five minutes, I'll call the police and charge you with trespassing."

Maude gave her a long, hard stare before apparently deciding she meant it. She pressed her lips together, took a deep breath, and expelled it, her chest rising and falling with the effort. "Very well. I felt it my duty to warn you. What happens next is your own fault."

Allie suppressed a shiver. She was only too aware of the strange things going on behind the paired doors of the old Queen Anne mansion. And this confrontation did nothing to steady her nerves.

Mary turned at the foot of the steps and looked back. She didn't say anything, but somehow her silent appraisal was more unnerving than Maude's ranting.

Cora took the key from Allie's limp hand. "Let's get inside. I've had enough dramatics for one day. I need my lunch and a nap, in that order.

Chapter Seven

Clay dropped by that afternoon. Allie answered the door, and he grinned down at her, thinking she looked a little ruffled. "I didn't have anything to do today, so I thought maybe we could look around outside and plan landscaping."

"Oh, Clay, I don't have money for landscaping. It will take everything I can scrape together to fix up the house."

He didn't tell her that landscaping didn't interest him much either. He just wanted to spend some relaxing time in her company. "Landscaping doesn't have to cost a mint. Come on outside. It's a pretty day, and the fresh air will do you good."

She smiled. "Sounds nice. Let me get a sweater, and I'll be right with you." They wandered through the front yard while Clay pointed out places to put flowerbeds. "Along the front of the house, maybe, and a climbing rose on the fence. What do you think?"

She wrinkled her nose, looking thoughtful. "Sounds good. I just hadn't gotten around to thinking about landscaping yet. But I know the outside has to look as good as the inside."

"What kind of plants do you want?"

"I don't have a clue. I'm not a plant person. Something that will go with the colors of the house, I guess. Maybe something that has pink or blue or white blooms, maybe a clear yellow. No red or orange. What do you think?"

"Sounds good to me. Cora raised lots of flowers at her old house. She can probably give you advice when it's time to make a choice."

Allie leaned against the wrought-iron fencing and gazed up

at her house. "I'm very lucky to have her. There is no way I could do this by myself."

"She's a fine woman." Clay agreed. "Cora Witner never did anyone a day's harm in her life."

"I don't see how her father and brother could have treated her that way."

"Well, Blakely's her half brother. His mother died, and old Homer married the first woman he could find, and they had Cora."

"She's had a hard life, apparently."

"Hard enough. Want to walk around to the back? The old carriage house needs some work. It's built solid. Mostly it just needs cleaning and some windowpanes replaced. Won't cost much," he added as she started to protest.

She laughed. "I guess I sound like a miser, but I only have a certain amount of money to spend."

"You sound like someone who's trying to start a business and is being responsible about spending." He'd help her all he could. Today was the first time they'd spent any time alone just talking. But it wouldn't be the last if he had anything to say about it. He was proud of her. She had grit. It had to be hard to stay in the face of so much harassment, but she was hanging in there. They sat down on an old cement garden bench. He was close enough to smell her perfume. Like flowers. Sweet but not overpowering. He liked that.

"Allie . . ."

"Clay . . ."

They spoke at the same time, then stopped and laughed. "You go first," he said.

"Cora and I went to church today."

"I saw you there."

"You were in church? I didn't see you."

"I was on the opposite side, two rows back. Probably got out before you did. Anything unusual happen?"

"I met Anna Milcrest. She wants to talk to me about Eliza."

He thought about that. "Seems to me the Milcrests and Ramsdales used to be good friends until Otis got himself arrested. She'd know about Eliza if anyone would. Are you interested in talking to her?"

She looked away from him. "The members of my family seem to have rejected Eliza. No one even went to her funeral. I want to know why."

"What difference could it make now? She's gone. Nothing can be changed."

"It's like a secret in some way, and I feel this need to understand."

"Sometimes old secrets are better left buried. What if you learn something that changes the way you feel toward this house?" He had a hunch the reason so many people wanted the house was rooted in the past, and he'd feel better if Allie stuck to restoring it and getting it ready to be a bed-and-breakfast until he could figure out a way to stop the harassment.

She shook her head. "I love this house. It feels like home. Like I'm supposed to be here. I guess that sounds silly."

"No, I'd say that sounds about right. It's a beautiful house, and you've put a lot of yourself into it. It's not just Eliza's house anymore. It's yours, and you're leaving your mark on it."

"I suppose that's what has Maude Wheeler and Mary Olson so upset. They were here today when we got home."

"What did they want?"

"Oh, the same old same old. Maude insisting that I'm to leave, the house really belongs to her. Mary doesn't say much, just protests that she has a stronger right to the house than Maude. She seems sort of intense."

"Mary?" He thought about it. "Maybe so. She's quieter, anyway. Don't let them spook you. They're just a nuisance."

"I know, but they get on my nerves."

Clay held up a hand. "Listen. I hear something."

Allie turned her head in the direction he indicated. "I hear it too—someone crying?"

"I'll go check on it. You wait here."

"Not a chance. I'm right behind you."

Clay walked slowly in the direction of the sound, stopping occasionally to get his bearings. "Well, would you look at that?"

A black pup with a white spot on its nose and a white underbelly was caught in a piece of woven wire, its head lodged firmly in one of the openings. From the looks of it, the dog had been there for some time. Clay worked gently until he freed the little animal from the wire prison. He stood up, holding it in his arms.

"Oh, a puppy. Where do you suppose it came from?"

"I have no idea," Clay said. "I'll try to find it a home."

"It has a home." Allie took the little body from him and scratched behind the floppy ears. "I like dogs, and it will be company for me."

When she's alone at night, he thought. The knowledge that someone could invade her sanctuary filled him with dread, but he didn't want to say anything that would scare her. "Okay, he's yours. We'd better take him back to the house and give him some warm milk. He looks half starved." Maybe the dog could warn her if someone was in the house.

Allie stroked the pup's head. "I'll take him to the vet to get him checked out. He's got a few bad cuts from the wire."

Clay opened the door for Allie and the pup. She carried it to the kitchen and put it on the floor, where it dropped down in a rumpled little heap, apparently exhausted by its ordeal.

"What can I feed it?" Allie asked.

As hungry as the pup looked, Clay figured anything would do. "What do you have? Milk? Meat? What's available?"

"A bowl of milk with bread and meat gravy mixed in—how does that sound?"

He made a face. "Repulsive, but then, I'm not a starving puppy. He'll probably like it."

She filled a bowl and set it down in front of the dog. It sniffed a couple of times and started eating, alternating between the food bowl and the pan of water Allie placed nearby. They watched in silent appreciation at the sight of something that really knew how to enjoy food. By the time the dish had been licked clean, the puppy's sides extended until he looked twice his original size. He flopped down next to the feed bowl and heaved a satisfied sigh.

Clay laughed. "Looks like he gained three pounds, doesn't he?"

Allie grinned. "I know the feeling. I can look at a piece of pie and gain a pound."

Clay shook his head. "Don't go thinking you need to lose weight. There's nothing wrong with the way you look."

She blushed and looked away. "I don't know how a dog will work with a bed-and-breakfast."

"Should be just fine. As long as he's housebroken, most people will take to him."

"I suppose." She leaned over and scratched the puppy's ears. "He's a good dog."

"You have any serious facts on which you're basing that opinion?"

She laughed. "He's my dog. That's the only fact I need."

"What are you going to name him?"

"I hadn't thought about a name. Any suggestions?"

"Rover? Shep?" he suggested.

She wrinkled her nose, shaking her head. "Nothing so commonplace for my dog."

"Pooch? Pup? No-Good Aggravating Hound?"

She laughed. "You're no help. I think I'll name him Midnight."

"Midnight? Do you have any idea how you'll sound yelling, 'Here, Midnight'?"

"Not good." She agreed. "How about . . . Taz?"

"Now, that's better. Taz it is."

The puppy opened one eye, as if agreeing with their choice, and then slumped over on its side, and in a few minutes they heard a muffled snore.

Clay leaned back in his chair. "Anything new happen I don't know about?"

Allie shook her head. "It's been quiet so far today. Just the visit by Maude and Mary. Are they related, by the way? They're always together."

"Not that I know. Maude may seem a bit eccentric, and she's got a group of followers, including some rather well-known people. She's got more influence than you'd think from listening to her. I'm not into cults myself, but you'd be surprised at the people who look to Maude for spiritual advice."

"What about Mary?"

"I think she's a relative newcomer. I don't remember seeing her around much, anyway. I guess she's a member of Maude's group."

Allie frowned. "Well, I don't care what kind of cult Maude's involved in. She's trying to run me out of my house, and I want her stopped."

"She's a nuisance, I'll agree, and if you want me to, I'll talk to her, not that I think it would do much good. She's not into listening. Particularly when it's against something she's already decided to do."

"And she's decided to take over my house."

Clay patted her hand. "This whole thing is just about her getting what she wants. She'll calm down when she realizes she's not going to get the house. I'm not going to let anyone take your home away from you, and that's a promise."

"You just want to make sure you get to finish working on it."

Clay tried to find a way to put it so it didn't scare her into running away. "That's part of it, sure. But it's not the main reason. I think a lot of you. I don't want to see anyone trying to push you around. I admire the way you're hanging in there, trying to make your dream come true."

She blinked, looking surprised. "I see. I think."

"Good. Now I'd better go. Got things to do. Take care of the pup."

She followed him to the door, and he turned to look back at her. "You call me if anything bothers you. Anything. You hear?"

She nodded, not speaking, but her eyes were warm and held his for a moment longer than necessary. He whistled on his way to the car.

Allie spent the rest of the afternoon going over the bills and tallying her checking account. Her mood was lighter than it would have been because of Taz. The puppy slept under the table with his head on her feet. The only time he moved was to waddle on short legs to the feed dish or his water bowl. Whenever Allie picked him up to cuddle, he was so full, he grunted, and his little pink tongue stuck out in total satisfaction.

After a light supper, which she ate in front of the television, she went upstairs to her room, with Taz laboring after her until she picked him up and carried him the rest of the way. He settled down for the night on an old blanket she'd placed in a corner. Allie stretched out on her bed, trying to avoid thinking about the attempts to drive her away. She couldn't quit and run now, even if she wanted to, which she didn't. She'd made promises to Clay and to Cora, and she had to keep them if at all possible. Taz whimpered in his sleep, and she glanced in his direction. He was another responsibility. Was she up to the job she had cut out for herself? She'd do the best she could and trust that everything would work out all right. After all, what other choice did she have?

The next morning Cora showed up to fix breakfast. They had decided that, since she would be in charge of meals when they opened for business, she might as well experiment at the house. Breakfast this morning was a casserole Allie would die for. Sausage, ham, eggs, cheese, and she didn't know what else, but it was wonderful.

"This is a definite addition to the menu." Allie spoke around a mouthful of casserole. "Is it an original recipe?"

"Just something I came up with," Cora said. "You like it?"

"I love it. Write down the ingredients before you forget them."

"Already done that. What are we doing today?"

"I thought we could clean the attic. That okay with you?"

"We might as well, I suppose. We have to get it done sometime. I'll fix beans and ham for lunch and bake a pan of jalapeño cornbread. Will that do?"

"Sounds good to me."

Taz waddled into the kitchen carrying an old tennis shoe of

Allie's. Cora stopped in the act of buttering a slice of toast. "What is that?"

"A puppy."

"I see that. Let me rephrase it. What is that dog doing in this kitchen?"

Allie scooped up the pup and wrinkled her nose at him. "Clay and I found him caught in wire at the back of the yard. I decided to keep him."

Cora watched in evident disapproval. "Well, as long as you don't expect me to take care of him. I am not a dog person."

Allie got up to fill his feed dish. "His name is Taz."

"I'll remember that. It might come in handy when I want to yell at him."

Allie laughed. "He's a *good* dog, he is."

"No need to get sloppy." Cora got up to clear the table. "If you want to go up and get started, I'll put lunch on, and then I'll join you."

"Good idea. I'll shut Taz up in my room so he won't be in the way."

"That's the smartest thing you've said so far." Cora dug through the refrigerator. "I thought I had some ham here." She found it, straightened, and stumbled over Taz. "Allie!"

"Right. We're going." Allie scooped up the pup and carried him upstairs to her room. He whined and scrabbled at the door as she left on her way to the attic, but she hardened her heart against his pleas. They had a lot of work to do, and he'd just be in the way. Besides, Cora hadn't taken to the idea of having a dog. She hoped it didn't become a problem.

The attic was a junk dealer's dream. Boxes of magazines, old books, discarded furniture. She wandered through the clutter, choosing items they might be able to use, but most of it could be sold, which would bring in money to use for operating expenses. She'd read it took five years to get a new business up and running. She didn't have enough money to hold out that long. Allie lifted the lid on an old trunk. Maybe she could find something here that would shed light on the problems between the family and Aunt Eliza.

Cora joined her, and they spent the morning clearing away the clutter, deciding what to keep, what to sell, and what to throw away, although Cora suggested they not dispose of anything until they gave a local antique dealer a chance to look at it.

"We don't know what's valuable and what isn't."

"Right." Allie held up a whalebone corset. "I doubt if anyone would want that."

"Don't be so sure. It might work for a museum or something."

" 'Something' covers it, all right." Allie placed it on the discard pile.

"Look at this," Cora said. "A photo album. Do you recognize anyone?"

"No, how could I?" But Allie bent over the photographs, searching. "Maybe Aunt Eliza is in here. I'd love to see what she looked like when she was young."

"Why not take it down to your room, and you can go over it when you have time."

"Good idea." Allie closed the book and looked at her watch. "I need to get cleaned up. I'm supposed to go to Anna's at two o'clock this afternoon."

"Oh, I forgot. Her daughter called. Anna isn't feeling well today. She asked if you'd mind putting it off until tomorrow. I said that'd be fine. Okay?"

"Sure. Whatever works for her works for me."

Allie lifted a box of books off a mahogany gate-legged table and almost dropped them. An old-fashioned music box with a pirouetting ballerina had been hidden from view. She turned the key, winding it, and the tinny notes of "Let Me Call You Sweetheart" drifted out into the room. So this was where the music had come from. Music boxes didn't wind themselves, so someone had been hiding in the attic that day. Somehow she had missed the intruder, which wasn't surprising, given all the hiding places up here.

Cora stopped working to listen. "I haven't heard that song in years."

Allie was tempted to tell her that she'd heard it all too recently, but it had happened before Cora came. No point in bringing it up.

They took time to clean up before Cora put the pan of jalapeño cornbread into the oven. Allie pored over the photograph album, with Taz asleep in her lap.

They were lingering over a Mrs. Smith's cherry cobbler Cora had shoved into the oven along with the cornbread when the phone rang. Allie answered.

"May I speak to Cora Witner?"

"Of course. Who's calling please?" Not that she was nosy, but she didn't trust Blakely.

"Roger Axelrod." His voice was sort of medium deep and casually friendly.

"Oh, yes. I'll get her."

She entered the kitchen. "It's for you. Roger."

Cora looked startled. "He'll ask me out to dinner. I don't know what to say."

"Say yes. Go on." Allie gave her a gentle shove. "Be nice to him. He seems like a nice man."

Cora left the room, looking as if she was heading to her own execution. Allie resisted the urge to eavesdrop. She did keep an eye on the clock, though, and it was a good five minutes before Cora returned, looking flushed and pleased.

"So you said yes?" Allie demanded.

Cora nodded. "We're going to the Bismarck."

"Way to go, girl." Roger must really be interested if he was springing for the Bismarck, Stony Point's most elegant restaurant, on a first date. "You go home and rest, take a nice, long bubble bath, and use plenty of perfume."

"I don't have perfume," Cora said. "No need to get all fussy. It's just two old friends having dinner together."

"Don't hand me that. I've got just the thing." Allie took the stairs two steps at a time, afraid to give Cora a chance to change her mind.

She scurried down to the kitchen and thrust a cluster of bottles into her friend's hand. "Here. Use these."

Cora looked at the labels. "What is all this?"

"Bubble bath, lotion, and perfume. You'll like it. More to the point, Roger will like it."

"Southern Night?" Cora read. "Oh, I don't think so. I don't like heavy perfumes."

"It's not heavy. Just roses, jasmine, a mere whiff of gardenia."

"I see. Sounds like a flower garden." Cora uncapped the lotion bottle. "Mmm. It does smell good."

"Told you." Allie placed her hands on Cora's shoulders and turned her toward the kitchen door. "Go on. Pamper yourself. I'll take care of the dishes."

After Cora left, time passed slowly. Clay came to install cabinets in the new bathroom. "Hey, you all by yourself?"

"I sent Cora home. She has a date with Roger Axelrod tonight. He's taking her to the Bismarck."

"He's a nice guy. They'll have a good time." He inched the cabinet into place. "You doing anything tonight?"

"No, not really." Her heart skipped a beat. Was he going to ask her out?

He edged the cabinet an inch to the right. "Since you're going to be here alone, why don't we catch a bite to eat at the Country Catfish all-you-can-eat buffet?"

"I can eat a lot of catfish. I wouldn't want to embarrass you."

He grinned at her. "I'm not that easily embarrassed, and I'm the catfish-eating 'champeen' of the Ozarks. Woman, you're up against powerful competition."

"The bigger they are, the harder they fall."

"Pick you up at five thirty?"

"Sounds good."

He left, and she decided to take her own advice. She had time for a long, soaking bath, shampoo, and manicure. Taz snuffled around her feet, and she scooped him up, holding him over her head. "I've got a date, big boy. What you think about that?"

She pulled him close, and he licked her chin. Amazing,

how one little puppy could make the house seem so much friendlier. She had a hunch keeping him was the smartest thing she'd ever done. Next to befriending Cora, that was.

Clay arrived a few minutes before five thirty, but she was ready and waiting. Taz had been fed and shut up in her bedroom. Although he voiced his complaints, he soon quieted down. She had dressed carefully in tan slacks, a cream T-shirt, and a tan jacket. Understated, simple, and, she hoped, elegant.

From the look in Clay's eyes, she had chosen wisely. He wore khaki pants and a beige shirt and dark brown jacket, which complemented his red hair and sherry brown eyes. One good-looking man. A little squiggle of anticipation coursed through her. She intended to put her troubles aside and enjoy this night.

The catfish was everything he had promised, and they both ate plenty, but she had to admit, she couldn't keep up with Clay. Coleslaw, crisp and tangy, was seasoned just right, and the hushpuppies had a zing of jalapeño. The waitress kept their iced tea glasses filled.

Allie pushed her plate aside. "I'm stuffed."

"Me too." Clay swigged the last of his tea. "We'll have to do this again."

Allie was surprised at how much she'd enjoyed herself. Clay was good company. He paid the bill, and they walked out to the car. He opened the door for her, which moved him up a notch in her estimation. She didn't remember Howard ever opening a door for her, although surely he had occasionally.

The drive home was quiet, but it was a peaceful quiet, as if a milestone had been passed and they were so comfortable with each other that they didn't have to talk. Allie leaned her head back against the seat, enjoying just being with Clay. He was a very restful person—strong, capable, and dependable. Superior qualities.

When they reached the house, Clay took the keys from her and unlocked the door. "Are you okay with being here alone?

Want me to go through the rooms and see if everything is all right?"

"No. I'm not afraid." So, okay, she was a little, but she had no intention of admitting it.

He nodded, but his expression showed doubts. "I'll see you tomorrow, then."

She nodded. "Tomorrow."

He waited as she went inside and closed the door. Before going upstairs, she took a quick tour of the downstairs, but everything seemed to be in order. She could hear Taz whining to get out of the bedroom, but it wasn't the agitated sound he made when something had disturbed him. She relaxed, realizing how tense her shoulders had been. Apparently her unknown intruder hadn't paid a visit tonight.

Allie had been asleep, but now she was wide-awake, staring into the darkness. Had something pulled her out of a sound slumber? She lay quietly for a few minutes before getting out of bed to go to the bathroom. When she opened the bedroom door, she was surprised to find the night-light had gone out.

She groped her way down the hall, wishing she'd thought to bring a flashlight. A faint ruffle of movement caught her attention. What was that? She held her breath, listening. A soft whisper of sound—someone breathing close at hand? Someone who was in the hall with her? She sensed a presence, coming closer. Allie inched backward, trying to reach her bedroom. If she could get inside, lock the door . . .

The darkness confused her. She stepped wrong, her foot coming down awkwardly, causing her to lose her balance. Her shoulder hit the wall, the soft thud loud in the silence. A sharp intake of breath, a rush of movement, waking Taz. The startled pup rushed from the bedroom, barking shrilly. Allie heard the swift patter of footsteps retreating down the stairs.

She caught Taz, holding him against her. He struggled for a minute and then relaxed. The night-light came back on, illuminating the empty hall. Allie carried Taz back to her bedroom and closed the door, then pushed a chair against it for good measure. She sank down onto her bed, nerves screaming in protest. Who had been in the hallway tonight? Was the intruder coming to her bedroom? What would have happened if she hadn't been awake? For the rest of the night, what little sleep she got, she got with the light on.

The raucous music of his cell phone woke Clay. He shook his head to clear it, trying to open up his thought process. Where had he left the thing? He cast a bleary look in the direction of the chest of drawers and saw the telephone halfway hidden beneath the shirt he had discarded last night.

By the time he reached the phone, it had rung five times and didn't show any sign of quitting. Flustered at being jerked violently awake, he growled into the receiver. "Hello."

Who could be calling at this hour? A glance at his watch showed him it wasn't all that early. In fact, he was running late. Very late. He'd spent most of the night lurking in the garden at the Ramsdale house, hoping to find out who was terrorizing Allie and Cora. Unfortunately the only thing he'd accomplished was loss of sleep.

"Hello, darling. In a bad mood this morning?"

Gilda. He sighed. "No, just in a hurry."

"Evidently you're a very busy man. I never see you anymore. Working on the Ramsdale house must be more time-consuming than I had suspected."

"It can be." He had no intention of going there. Any way he answered that comment would just get him into deep water. "What can I do for you?"

"Oh, lots of things, but we won't go into that now. I wondered if you were free for dinner tonight. I feel domestic."

Now, there was a loaded sentence if he'd ever heard one. Conversation with Gilda was becoming increasingly more like walking through a minefield.

"Oh, hey, I'm sorry. I can't make it tonight."

"How about tomorrow night?"

"It looks like I'm going to be busy all week."

"Little Miss McGregor doesn't seem to have any trouble getting you to spend time with her. Did you enjoy your catfish dinner?"

So she'd heard about that. "Look, Gilda. Allie is just a friend. We went out to dinner once. It didn't mean anything."

"Just like those dinners you had with me didn't mean anything?" He heard a hard, tight note in her voice. "I get it. You wanted answers about the house and the new owner. I was just an information source to you. Now that you have the job, you think you don't need me any longer. Is that it?"

"Why would I care what's going on at the Bailey & Grant law office?" he demanded. "That doesn't make sense."

"It does when one considers how much you want that house on your resume. So much, you'll even take up with little Miss McGregor if the house comes with her."

"Is that what you think of me?" Clay demanded.

"Oh, that doesn't even begin to say what I think of you," Gilda lashed out. "If you believe you can use me and then walk away, you have another think coming."

"Look, Gilda. We've always been just friends. There wasn't anything more between us."

"I see. I'm not going to dignify this conversation by pointing out that I had every right to assume we were building something with meaning. Evidently you saw it differently. Well, little Miss McGregor had better be careful. A man who's allergic to commitment isn't much of a bargain."

"There's no point in continuing this," Clay began.

"My opinion, exactly, *darling*!"

Five minutes later his head was still ringing from the sound of the receiver being slammed down in his ear.

After a makeshift breakfast Clay decided to go to the grocery store. A quick look inside the refrigerator reinforced this decision. Unless he wanted to dine on a can of Diet Pepsi and a dried-out orange, it was time to stock up.

Business at the store was booming, and he maneuvered down the aisles, trying to dodge a couple of young boys playing demolition-derby with grocery carts. Their mad dashes toward each other, accompanied by the clanging of colliding metal, went unchecked except for the absent murmurings of a wan young woman paying more attention to the freshness of the produce than the activities of her two sons.

Clay ducked down the cereal aisle with the notion of picking up something easy for breakfast and came face-to-face with Maude Wheeler. Her mouth gaped open in surprise, then closed in a way that reminded him of the snapping turtle that lived at the bottom of his garden.

"You!" A mottled red flush stained her cheeks.

"Uh . . . yeah." He tried to edge past, but she moved to block him.

"I've seen the way you are desecrating that house, painting it the wrong color. The spirits are very disturbed."

"Now, Maude . . ."

"Don't you 'Now, Maude' me. Turning that lovely home into a bed-and-breakfast. How dare you?"

"Well, it's like this. . . ."

"And that McGregor woman! What business does she have with a house like that? It was meant for something better. I, and only I, have a right to live there. It is ordained."

"Now, Maude. You know Allie McGregor is the legal heir of Miss Eliza. It's her house, and there's nothing you can do about it. She's got a right to do what she pleases with it."

"No, she doesn't. That's what I've been trying to tell you. I lived in that house in a former life. I have a prior claim that comes from before Otis and Eliza Ramsdale. It is my house. Allie McGregor is the interloper whose claim must be denied by anyone with a thought to what is right and fair."

Clay sighed. "Maude, you know better than that. You didn't live a previous life. We both grew up in this town. I've known you for years. You made a lot more sense before you got mixed up in this junk."

Maude's voice rose to an alarming decibel. " 'Junk'! You dare call the beliefs of the enlightened 'junk'? I'll file a restraining order against you, stopping work on that house. I'll sue! I'll . . ."

"You'll do no such thing, and I've had enough of these hysterics. Give it up, Maude. What Allie McGregor does with that house is none of your business."

He left the store so angry, he forgot to buy groceries. Fine. He'd eat out. Maude's last words were still ringing in his ears. "I know you and that girl would like to get rid of me, but I will prevail. I will overcome. The infidels will be driven out of my house."

When that woman got an idea into her head, there was no stopping her. Half of Stony Point must have been in the store this morning. And they had all heard her temper tantrum. His ears burned with embarrassment. He should have walked away the moment he saw her, instead of trying to be polite. Next time he'd know better.

Chapter Eight

Allie dressed with care for her visit with Anna. The Milcrest house was charming. Built in the Second Empire style, it reminded her of an elegant wedding cake. The three-story square house with a projecting center pavilion crowned by ornamental iron cresting was the prettiest house on the street. Scrolled brackets supported the eaves, and the east elevation featured an impressive bay framed by wooden panels and molded cornices. She paused for a moment, gazing upward, imagining Eliza and Anna as young women, mistresses of their charming homes.

A fresh-faced teenager met her at the door. "Miss McGregor? I'm Kady. Grandma Anna is waiting for you in the library."

She led the way to an elegant room where Anna waited, seated in an overstuffed, comfortable-looking chair. "Forgive me for not getting up, child. My hip is bothering me today."

"That's okay. If you're not well, I could come back another time." Allie looked around the room, at the gold-tinted walls, the black and gold valances over sheer curtains tied back with gold roping.

"No, it will do me good to talk. I assume you've met my granddaughter, Kady."

Allie smiled. "Yes, we met at the door."

"She's going to bring us something to drink. Will iced tea be all right?"

"Of course, if it's not too much bother."

"No bother at all," Kady said. "Be back in just a minute."

They talked about the weather, about the community, just inconsequential chatter until Kady returned with iced tea and a plate of delicate lemon cookies dusted with confectioner's sugar.

Allie bit into one and closed her eyes in ecstasy. "I would love to have the recipe for these if it's not a secret. We could make them for our bed-and-breakfast."

" 'We'?" Anna asked. "You have a partner?"

"Cora Witner. She's living in the guesthouse now."

"Oh, yes. I heard about the perfectly dreadful way Homer and Blakely treated her. Cora's a very good woman. She'd have had to be, to put up with those two for all those years. I'll see you get the recipe."

Anna dusted the confectioner's sugar from her hands. "Now, let's get down to business. I do get tired easily, one of the drawbacks of age, and I want to talk to you about Eliza."

She reached over to the table beside her chair and picked up a photograph, which had been lying facedown. "This is what she looked like when she was young."

Allie stared at a young woman dressed in vintage clothing. Her hair was piled on top of her head, giving her an air of maturity belied by the laughing glint in her eyes and the lovely curve of her lips. "She's beautiful."

Anna sighed. "She really was. And so much fun. No matter how down I was, Eliza could always cheer me. I miss her so much."

"I wish I could have known her better. I came to see her once, but she wouldn't let me into the house. Didn't want me there."

"The old Eliza would have taken you in with open arms," Anna said. "She was always laughing, so full of love and compassion. All that left her when Otis was arrested and convicted."

"Was he really a jewel thief?"

Anna shrugged her shoulders. "I don't know. The police provided the evidence, but Eliza never believed he was guilty. She fought for him until the day he died, trying to clear his name and get him released. After she buried him, she seemed to have buried all her interest in life too. I guess she'd invested so much in trying to free him, she didn't have anything left."

"Anna, I didn't know about Eliza until right before I came to see her. What happened between her and my family?"

Anna twisted her lips in a charming moue. "They're your family, darling. What can I say?"

"You can tell me the truth. What caused the rift?"

"Well, they were a proud, stiff-necked bunch, and Eliza was proud too. They thought Otis was guilty."

"I see."

"She expected them to support her and help find out what she believed to be the truth, that Otis was framed, and they deserted her."

"But she needed them." To Allie it seemed tragic that the family she had always known and loved had rejected one of their own in this calloused way.

"I know. But they didn't consider her to be one of them, you know."

"No. I didn't know anything about that." Allie realized how little she actually knew concerning this aunt who had left her so much.

"I think she was a distant relative. Her parents died, and the McGregors took her in, but she never believed they wanted her."

Allie thought about that. Poor Eliza. She must have felt she didn't belong anywhere. "What was Otis like?"

"Otis? He was a nice enough man, rather dull, but he adored Eliza. They went on trips, had fun."

"Where did they get the money?"

"He was a good businessman. Money wasn't a problem for them."

"What did he do?"

Anna smiled and shook her head. "You really don't know anything about them, do you?"

"No. For the longest time I never even knew they existed. I was at a family party, and one of my aunts had been to Stony Point, and someone asked if she'd seen Eliza, and they laughed. It made me curious."

Anna's eyes glinted with anger. "Laughed at Eliza? When she was worth more than all of them put together." She made an obvious effort to get herself under control. "Otis owned the mercantile, an auto dealership, had an interest in the bank and a couple of restaurants. Everything the man touched turned a profit. Eliza had to sell it all, of course, when he was convicted. She spent a lot of money trying to get him free, and then when he died in prison, she just retired behind the walls of that house and didn't see anyone much, except me."

"Anna, why did she leave me the house?"

"Two reasons. One, because you came to see about her. Even though she refused to let you in, she was touched. And because of this." She picked up a cardboard expanding file. "This is for you."

Allie took the file and turned it over in her hands. "What is it?"

"All the information she collected about Otis' trial. She wanted you to clear his name."

"She did what?" The words jolted out of Allie. "How could she expect me to do that? The case is ancient by now."

"Old and cold," Anna agreed, that mischievous sparkle back in her eyes. "Eliza wasn't real sensible where Otis was concerned. She loved him very much."

Despite the picture Anna had shown her, Allie had a hard time seeing the frail, dried-up Eliza Ramsdale she'd met as a passionate woman who'd fought to clear her husband's name. "Still . . . I don't know what I can do."

"Neither do I, but Eliza had confidence in you. She said you were stubborn."

Allie managed a reluctant smile. "I suppose I am. And she did leave me her house. I guess I owe her."

Anna grinned. "Yes, she counted on that."

Clay had been at the Ramsdale house all afternoon, working on the shower in the new second-floor bathroom. Allie had insisted on keeping the old claw-foot tub in the other bathroom, so he only had this shower to install. It had taken him a while, but he finally had it working.

He gathered his tools and went downstairs. Cora was in the

kitchen, and he looked in to tell her he was leaving. She pushed a rolling pin over a lump of dough. "Why don't you stay for dinner? I'm trying out recipes. We're tinkering with the idea of maybe providing an evening meal, by reservation only, for our guests."

Clay sniffed the air. "Smells good. What's cooking?"

"A new chicken and dressing dish, mashed potatoes with roasted garlic, green beans, and peach pie, if I ever get it into the oven. That phone has been ringing all afternoon. I've made a dozen trips to the parlor. Allie called the telephone company, and they're supposed to install new lines next week, and I'll surely be glad."

"Where's she putting the new lines?"

"One here, one in the office, one in her bedroom, and one in the guesthouse."

"Good. I'll feel better if she can call out without having to come all the way downstairs at night."

"Me too." Cora deftly flipped the crust over and placed it in the pan. "Clay, who do you think is trying to scare her into leaving?"

"I don't know. I've thought about it often enough, but I can't come up with a single person who would benefit from Allie's leaving except Maude Wheeler and George Aiken."

Clay absently took a slice of peach from the bowl where Cora was mixing fruit for her pie, and she slapped his hand. "Stay out of there. I need those."

"Sorry." He grinned at her, then sobered as he returned to the topic under discussion. "I've known Maude for years. Well, so have you. Would you say she'd sneak around like that?"

Cora dumped the fruit into the pan and covered it with a second crust. She crimped the edges and smeared the top with cream, adding a sprinkle of sugar before replying. "No. I really can't. I've tried to believe she was behind it, but it's not her way."

"No," Clay agreed. "There's nothing devious about Maude. She just charges ahead, sure she's right, and she doesn't care who she storms over in the process."

"That about covers it. She'll show up here demanding Allie leave, and she'll tell all over town how she used to live here in another life and Allie stole the house from her, but I can't see her slipping around moving things and writing messages on mirrors."

The front door opened, and a few minutes later Allie appeared in the kitchen doorway. "What smells so good?"

"Chicken and dressing," Cora said.

"And peach pie. I'm staying for supper," Clay added.

Allie smiled. "Good. I need to talk to both of you anyway."

Clay thought she looked upset again, an expression she wore all too often to suit him. "How'd your visit go with Anna?"

"Just fine. She's a wonderful person." Allie pulled out a chair and sat down, placing an expanding file on the table.

"What did she tell you about Eliza?"

Cora, standing at the sink, turned around to listen. Allie shrugged. "She really loved Eliza. I wish I could have known her. It feels like I've been cheated in some way."

She opened the file. "Anna gave me this. It's all the information Eliza gathered about Otis' trial. According to Anna, Eliza never believed he was guilty. She worked to get him set free until he died in prison."

Clay didn't like the sound of that. "Why did she give it to you?"

Allie lifted her chin, meeting his gaze. "She wanted me to clear his name."

"You'll do no such thing." Clay hadn't realized he'd spoken until the words sort of hung in the air. From the expression on Allie's face, he knew he'd gone too far. "I mean, I hope you won't try to do that."

"Good backpedal," Cora murmured. "Not good enough, though."

"Are you giving me an order?" Allie asked.

"No. I wouldn't dream of it. But just listen, will you? If Otis wasn't guilty, although a jury of his peers convicted him, then someone else was. And that person let Otis take the rap. What if he's still alive today? You think he'll be happy if you show up riding a white horse, so to speak, ready to expose him after all these years?"

"If there's someone out there who put Eliza and Otis through that, even if he's old, then I don't care if he's happy or not. I want him punished. Are you going to help me?"

He met the challenge in her eyes and sighed. "Yes. I guess I am."

Allie woke up in the night and turned on her bedside lamp. Taz opened one eye and peered at her as she got out of bed and went down the hall to the bathroom, leaving the door ajar. If she shut him in, he would just cry until she returned. On her way back she stopped on the landing, holding her breath and listening but hearing nothing. The house seemed peaceful tonight, without that curious, listening air it had sometimes.

An eruption of barking and snarls interrupted her, followed by the startled yelp of an obviously agitated puppy. Allie broke for the bedroom door. Taz danced around the bed, threatening mayhem. In the middle of Allie's bed sat a beautiful gray and white long-haired cat eyeing the bouncing, yapping pup with perfect aplomb. The cat turned sea green eyes on Allie, as aloof as royalty inspecting a commoner. She gripped the door frame. Where had this cat come from?

Allie gingerly pushed the cat off the bed, wondering if it would scratch her. As soon as it hit the floor, Taz charged, only to get a lightning-fast slash across the tip of his tender nose. He yelped in pain and retreated under the bed, where he cowered, growling low in his throat. The cat ignored him. As Allie watched, the intruder lightly leaped back onto her bed and eyed her contemptuously. She placed her hands on her hips and glared back.

"Now look here, cat. I have no idea where you came from, but this is my room, and I don't like cats. Particularly when they creep in and take over."

It was the word *creep* that did her in. Where *had* the blasted thing come from? She had locked up herself, leaving no possible entrance for anything. She'd been all over this house too.

That cat had not been in the house today. She would swear to that. So where had this feline intruder come from, and how did it get into her bedroom? And just what was she supposed to do with a cat? Poor Taz was already a nervous wreck. She couldn't expect him to share his new home with a gray and white terror who could render him into a quivering mass of jelly with one malevolent glance.

Finally she lifted the cat from the bed and put it out of the room, closing the door firmly in its face. Taz, confident his enemy had been vanquished, marched stiff-legged toward the door, ready to do battle.

"You come back here, or I'll open the door and let the cat in," Allie threatened.

The pup shot her a disgusted look and wandered over to his blanket, where he slumped down and rested his head on his paws, worn out from defending his territory.

Allie turned out the light, but it was a long time before she could go to sleep for wondering how that cat had gotten into her house.

The next morning Cora arrived from the guesthouse and raised her eyebrows. "What have we here?"

"A cat."

"I'm aware of that. Why is it that you keep bringing animals home? Do you have a secret desire to own a zoo?"

"Very funny. I went to the bathroom last night, and when I got back to my room, that *cat* was sitting on my bed."

Cora fumbled for a chair. "It was in the house?"

"Right." Allie wearily reached down to swat the cat away from Taz's feed dish. "Your dish is over there. Go eat."

The cat shot her an insolent glance and walked over to rub its back against Cora's ankles. Allie stared at it in disbelief. "That cat likes you!"

"Understandable. I'm a likable person."

"Don't push it. I have run interference between cat and dog until I'm worn out. They hated each other on sight."

Cora lifted the cat and placed it on her lap, where it settled down and immediately began to purr. "It's a beautiful animal.

Surely it belongs to someone. I'll put it outside, and maybe it will go home."

She carried the cat to the back door and set it down on the step, shutting the door on a plaintive wail. "Let me wash my hands, and I'll fix breakfast. I thought maybe French toast."

"That sounds good." A few minutes later Allie got up from the table and stretched. She glanced toward the door and stopped with her arms over her head, frozen into position. "Cora?"

"What?"

"Look there."

The cat strolled into the room and stopped beside her feed dish, lapping milk with as much dignity as if she hadn't just been unceremoniously dumped outside.

Allie sat on the front porch reading through Eliza's file. She needed to put it into some sort of order. For the time being she was just taking a page out, reading it, and putting it back. Most of it didn't make sense to her. One more reason she needed to get it organized.

The cat was still in the house. Why bother to put it out when it could come and go at will? She and Cora had searched until they were worn out without finding a place where it could get in. Finally she had surrendered to the inevitable and let it stay.

She glanced up from the paper she held and saw an older man walking up her drive. He stopped at the foot of the stairs. Thin but not frail, seeming in good shape, judging from the ropy muscles in his arms. White hair, pale blue eyes. He tipped his hat. Polite.

"Good morning, ma'am."

Allie nodded, giving him time to state his business.

"My name's Harry Dalton. I'm looking for work."

"I see. What kind of work?"

"Anything. You name it, I can fix it. I'm retired—just got my Social Security check and a little pension. The place I've been staying has sold, and I've got to move. Heard you were fixing to open a bed-and-breakfast. You'll need someone to take care of this big yard and do maintenance."

Allie shook her head. "I'm sorry. I don't have anywhere for you to stay." She would need someone to help around the place once they opened, but that wouldn't be for a few weeks. Still . . . he looked healthy, and he needed work.

He turned the hat brim in his hands. "It wouldn't take much for me. Just someplace to sleep. I'm not fussy."

Allie watched him, compassion tugging at her heart "Well, there is a carriage house, but it's not in the greatest shape."

"Would it be all right if I looked at it?"

She hesitated. After all, she didn't know this man, but he seemed honest enough. *Jumping to conclusions, Allie?* She could just hear Howard making that comment. He claimed she was no judge of character, taking people at face value. Just for that, she'd talk to this Harry Dalton. Show Howard and everyone else that she was in charge.

"Wait until I put these things away, and we'll take a look." She got up from the porch swing and carried Eliza's clutch of papers inside, locking them in the desk drawer, where they would be safe from prying eyes unless their prowler had a key to the desk.

Harry was still waiting at the foot of the steps when she went back out onto the porch. Allie was having second thoughts about this venture. After all, she didn't know anything about this man. She glanced at him and found he was studying her with the same intensity. If he was out of a job and a home at his age, she guessed he had a reason to be uncertain. All right, she had agreed to show him the carriage house. No backing out now.

She had forgotten how forlorn the building was. Located behind and to the right of the house and guesthouse, it had been the object of neglect. There had been so many things to fix and money so tight, the carriage house had slipped to the bottom of her list. She unlocked the door, and they stepped inside. At least it wasn't crammed full of junk. Dirty veils of cobwebs dangled from the ceiling, filthy doilies long abandoned and forgotten by the creatures that had woven them. Allie's fingers itched for a broom. Whether Harry stayed here or not, she'd clean this place, make it presentable.

He stood in the middle of the room, looking around. "It's not too bad."

"It is, and you know it. I wouldn't put a dog in here."

He smiled. "Clean down those webs and sweep it out, and it'll look better."

"But not livable."

Harry strode across the room to an open door. He stopped in the doorway, peering inside. "There's already a bathroom down here, and this would be one big room for living. All I'd need is a hot plate and a refrigerator."

"You'd eat your meals at the house." Now, why had she said that? She hadn't hired him yet, although he apparently thought she had.

He climbed the stairs, and she waited, hearing him walking overhead. She looked around the dingy room, seeing possibilities. Not where *she* would want to live, but then, she wasn't as desperate as he seemed to be.

Harry descended the stairs. "Nice-sized room up there. Make a fine bedroom. I'll check the wiring and plumbing and get everything in working order. Won't cost much, since I'll do all the work myself. I don't have to move until the end of the week, and I'll have it in shape by then."

"We haven't talked about job description and salary yet."

"Oh, that's all right," he said cheerfully. "As long as I'm getting room and board, I won't expect much in the way of salary. Those two things can take a bite out of a Social Security check."

"I guess so." She hesitated. "You'll need a key."

"You keep that one for the time being. I can ask for it at the house when I need it."

She nodded, noticing how he countered all of her comments.

He patted her shoulder. "I realize you don't know anything

about me, but it'll be all right. I promise. Now I'll go buy a broom and some cleaning tools."

"You can get a broom from the house, and I can give you cleaning supplies." If he was willing to clean up this mess, she could at least provide the means.

They walked back to the house to pick up supplies, and Allie wondered uneasily how Cora would feel about this new employee. What with stray dogs and cats and handymen showing up unannounced on her doorstep, she was beginning to feel overwhelmed herself.

Harry followed her inside, looking around with apparent admiration on his face. "Now, isn't this something? Don't often see anything quite this fancy."

Cora came out of the parlor wearing an expression of surprise. "The telephone company called. They'll be here this afternoon to install new lines."

"Good. I suppose we'll need one in the carriage house too."

"We will?" Cora asked, her tone of voice as pointed as a stiletto.

Allie raised her chin. "Yes, we will. This is Harry Dalton. He'll be living in the carriage house and doing maintenance work at our bed-and-breakfast."

"Which we haven't opened yet."

"We will soon."

Cora unbent a little. "Nice to meet you, Harry. I believe the carriage house is rather dirty, isn't it?"

"Nothing a little work won't remedy," Harry assured her. "Miss Allie said you could spare me some cleaning supplies, but if that's a problem, I can buy my own."

"No, quite all right. Come out to the kitchen, and I'll find you something to use."

Allie watched them walk away. They reminded her of the cat and Taz. Cora, of course, was the cat. She felt sorry for Harry if he ever crossed Cora. Something else bothered her. When had she told Harry Dalton her name?

Cora and Harry had gone out to the carriage house, and Allie went upstairs to check on Taz, who had chosen hiding under the bed in the safety of her room over sharing the kitchen with a marauding cat.

She came downstairs and entered the parlor to find Mary Olson standing with her back to the door, looking around with a proprietary expression her face. Allie watched Mary's reflection in the mirror as she paused with one hand resting on the blue chair, head erect. The lady of the house?

Their eyes met in the mirror, and Mary blushed. "I'm sorry. I didn't see you there."

Allie nodded. "I didn't hear the doorbell."

"Oh, I didn't ring," Mary said. "I called, and when you didn't answer, I just came in looking for you."

Allie pretended to accept this explanation, although she didn't believe a word of it. Mary hadn't seemed interested in finding anyone. She had been behaving as if she lived here. Acting out a fantasy?

Mary glanced around the room again. "I don't care what Maude says, you're doing a good job fixing this place up. Eliza would be pleased."

"You knew Eliza?"

"Oh, yes, I knew Eliza." Mary's face set in rigid lines; her blue eyes glittered. Allie suspected she hadn't liked Eliza.

"How long have you lived in Stony Point?"

Mary didn't answer. Her eyes looked past Allie, her features twisted as if she were afraid.

The cat strolled into the room and stopped.

"That cat!"

The cat bristled, fur expanding until it looked twice its size. It crouched, shoulders hunched, as if ready to pounce.

"You . . . cat!" Mary gasped.

At the sound of her voice the cat streaked out the door, headed for the stairs in a gray and white blur. Its claws scrabbled on the worn wood of the steps.

Mary stared at Allie. "That's Dinah. Where did you find her?"

"I didn't. She found me. You know the cat?"

"I can't believe she's shown up. She's been gone for so long, I thought something had happened to her."

"Who does she belong to?" Allie asked. "If I can catch her, I'll take her home." That had been one scared cat.

"I wonder where she's been." Mary turned her head to look at the door as if she expected the feline to return. "That's Dinah . . . Eliza's cat."

Chapter Nine

Clay parked in front of the house in his usual place and got out, breathing in the fresh spring air. He loved spring and fall in the Ozarks. You could keep the temperamental winters and humid summers, but spring and autumn were special. Allie waved to him from the porch, and he started to stroll that way, when he became aware of a stranger walking around the side of the house carrying a hammer and a sack of what he took to be nails.

Clay watched the man move out of sight before climbing the porch steps to face Allie. He yanked a thumb in the direction in which the stranger had disappeared. "Who was that?"

"Harry Dalton. He's our new handyman."

Clay tried to keep the irritation out of his voice. "What's he handy at?"

"He claims he can fix anything. I'll need someone to do maintenance and yard work when we open up."

"What's he going to do until then?"

"Fix up the carriage house so he can live there."

"You're letting him move onto the place? Allie, what are you thinking? You're having all sorts of odd things happen, and you're letting a stranger move in?"

"I hardly think Harry's been the one sneaking around the house moving things."

"He could be the one who made the phone calls."

Clay noticed with satisfaction that that had stopped her. She stared up at him with a touch of near panic on her face. "I never thought of that."

104

"Well, maybe you should have."

Fire glowed in her eyes. "I'll remind you, this is my house and my business, and I can hire anyone I choose."

So there. She didn't say the words, but she might as well have. They were present in the tone of her voice. "Look, Allie. I'm sorry if I sounded like I was trying to tell you what to do. It's just that I'm worried about you. This harassment seems to be picking up. I'm afraid it'll get out of hand, and I don't want you to get hurt."

Her expression softened. "I know. It's just that I'm so tired of people telling me what I can and can't do. I'm not stupid."

"I never thought you were. You're smart enough to open a business and make it work, if we can find out what's going on and put a stop to it. You can't have guests in a house where things keep moving around. People may laugh about ghosts, but they don't want to live with one."

"I don't believe in ghosts."

"Neither do I, but some people do."

The cat stalked around the front of the house and walked past Clay, head erect, bearing royal. Clay stared after it, mouth open, before turning to look at Allie. "What is that?"

Her expression was entirely too smug. She grinned. "Meet Dinah, Eliza Ramsdale's cat. The queen has returned."

Clay still felt stunned. "A dog, a handyman, and now a cat. The place is turning into a zoo."

"Cora's words, exactly."

"When did the cat show up? It hasn't been here while we've been working—I'm sure of that."

Allie stopped looking so pleased. "It just appeared last night. In my room. I haven't any idea how or why, it was just there."

"What are you going to do with it?"

"I have no idea. If it's Eliza's cat, and Mary Olson says it is, then it belongs here. It will all work out, I suppose."

Cora opened the screen door and stepped outside. "Hi, Clay. I thought I heard you out here. Have you seen our new maintenance man?"

"From a distance. What do you think of him?"

"He's a worker. Got that carriage house swept and mopped, and I'll have to admit it looks better. Good manners. I guess he'll do."

"I've also met the cat." Clay glanced over to where Dinah had stretched out in a patch of sunlight. "She seems to feel at home."

"I've been thinking about that," Cora said. "The cat and that dog don't get along."

"Dinah," Allie said.

Cora stopped and looked at her. "What did you say?"

"I said, Dinah. That's her name, according to Mary Olson."

"Oh, yes? And how does Mary know that?"

"I have no idea. But she said it was Eliza's cat, and she'd come back."

"I see. Well, that doesn't change anything. I'm taking the cat to stay with me at the guesthouse, if you have no objections."

"None at all," Allie assured her. "But why?"

"I've always liked cats, but I never had one. This . . . Dinah . . . seems to like me, and I just thought it would put an end to the fighting. I'm beginning to feel sorry for that pup. He's afraid to eat from his own bowl."

Clay left them discussing the advantages and disadvantages of color-coordinated towels for each room and wandered back to the carriage house.

Harry Dalton looked up from dabbing putty around a new windowpane. "Afternoon."

"See you're getting it into shape," Clay said.

"Trying to. Don't need much work, just cleaning up and a few repairs. Walls and roof are sound."

Clay watched him finish the window. He seemed to know what he was doing. Anyway, as Allie pointed out, it wasn't any of his business.

Harry glanced at him. "I guess you're wondering about me."

"I was just curious why you came here looking for work."

"The other morning I was having a cup of coffee, and I

heard that Wheeler woman mouthing off about Miss McGregor opening a bed-and-breakfast. I figured I might get in on the ground floor, so to speak, so I hurried over here and asked for a job."

"I see. Well, you're doing good work on that window."

"Thanks. I've worked in construction most of my life."

"Ever done any restoration work?"

"No, nothing that fancy. Just plain construction."

Clay nodded. "Well, I've bothered you long enough. Good to meet you."

He walked away relieved that Harry Dalton knew his business, but he still didn't feel completely satisfied about the older man. Maybe he could check around town, find out more about him.

Cora had gone home for the night, and Allie closed and locked up. Not that it did any good. Evidently someone had the freedom to come and go, although she had yet to discover how and where. She took her bath and settled down in bed to spread out the papers in Eliza's file. It was time she tried to make sense of them. One by one she took out the printed sheets and read them carefully, looking for something to back up Eliza's belief in her husband's innocence. Gradually a pattern formed, and she sorted the sheets into separate piles according to date and data.

One paper jammed into the bottom of the file resisted her efforts to remove it. Finally she upended the cardboard file and gave it a hard shake. The folded sheet tumbled out and fluttered just out of reach. Annoyed, Allie, tossed the file aside and stretched across the blanket to retrieve the wayward sheet of paper. The format revealed it was a letter. She glanced at the signature at the end. From Eliza. Intrigued, she started at the beginning.

Dear Allison:
You will be surprised to learn I've left you this house.
I've regretted not letting you in the day you came to visit.

I have no excuse for my rudeness, except the bitterness I have harbored in my heart for far too long. When my husband was arrested for a crime he did not commit, my family turned their backs on me.

I should have expected it, since they have never considered me to be a legitimate part of the family. My parents died when I was thirteen, and as I had no one else, my Aunt Valen and Uncle Todd took me in. Perhaps I was too old and too grief-stricken to adjust, or, perhaps, as I believed, they considered me an unwanted burden. At any rate it was a relief to all when I married and moved away.

You will hear that my husband was a thief, but that is false. Otis Ramsdale never stole anything from anyone in his entire life. He was a respected businessman who earned his place in society. I can't say the same about his family. It is my belief that his brother James, who looked very similar, impersonated Otis and stole those jewels.

I have given much of my life to trying to prove my husband's innocence, to no avail. I am hoping you will take up the task. I realize you have no obligation to do so, but I am counting on your well-developed sense of responsibility. I believe you have this trait, because you came to check on me and continued to send cards at Christmas and Easter. No one else ever bothered. I know I am imposing on you, but you are my last chance to clear my husband's name. You can walk away from this request if you choose, and the house will still be yours. I prefer to believe you will stay the course.

Eliza Ramsdale

Allie refolded the letter and held it for a moment, staring into space. As much as she wanted to honor Eliza's request and regardless of how she had stressed her determination to do so, she knew she had very little chance for success. Too much time had passed, and the main participants were probably dead.

She unfolded the letter again, searching for a name. *James Ramsdale.* Older than Otis or younger? Either way, someone must remember him. Would he really have let his brother go to prison in his stead? According to Eliza, she suspected him of manipulating the evidence to throw suspicion onto Otis. Whatever happened to brotherly love? Maybe Anna Milcrest would know something about James. At the very least she might be able to suggest where to start looking for members of Otis' family. Surely he had living relatives somewhere. Although Aunt Eliza didn't seem to think highly of them. Allie remembered her father saying something similar. Had the family felt Eliza had married beneath them? Was that why they were so quick to disown her when Otis was arrested? No matter what the reason, the way they had deserted her didn't reflect too well on them.

Allie gathered up the papers, trying to keep them in some sort of order. A new thought occurred to her. John Bailey had known her aunt. He might very well be able to advise her on this situation. She wondered if he knew of the request Eliza had made. Probably. But if so, he was too discreet to hand out advice until she asked. She placed the file on the bedside table and turned out the light.

Outside her window she could see stars gleaming against the night sky. She loved this house more every day. When things calmed down, she wanted to have her parents come for a few days, but not until they had solved the mystery of the moving objects. Her mother preferred romances to mysteries.

Which brought her to the problem of Howard and her parents. She knew they liked him and looked forward to having him for a son-in-law, but they had never seen him as he really was. Howard had manipulation down to a fine art. He could be charming, fun, and exciting, as long as he was the center of attention. It was all about him. Everyone else was reduced to polishing that image. Well, she had plumb run out of polish. A lifetime of playing fetch didn't appeal to her.

She closed her eyes, listening to Taz snoring contentedly from his blanket beside her bed. It would be nice if they could make it through the night without more problems, but she knew there was no guarantee of that. After a moment's thought, she got out of bed and brought a straight-backed chair from one of the other bedrooms, propping it under the doorknob. At least if someone tried to enter, the sound might wake her. She grinned at the sleeping puppy. At any rate, it would wake him. Not much got past Taz, the guard dog.

Clay rubbed his eyes and blinked at the glowing computer screen. Otis Ramsdale had been a respected businessman, loving husband, and a deacon in the First Baptist Church until he was arrested for being a jewel thief. Had he really fooled so many people for so long? It hardly seemed possible. He had no trouble finding Otis on the Internet. A search had turned up several sites. He'd even found copies of newspaper articles about the trial and had printed them for Allie to read later. Otis had cut a wide swath in Stony Point and surrounding areas. He'd been a good-looking man, medium height, brown hair, and light blue eyes, according to one description.

A new idea occurred to Clay. He switched to a genealogy search, looking for a family tree. A search for Otis Ramsdale turned up several sites, but none that appeared promising. He was too tired to look anyway. The clock read 11:15. Clay yawned and stretched. Time to pack it in. Now that he was interested, he'd do some more searching tomorrow night. Maybe he could stumble upon something that would warrant opening the case again, but he doubted it. Too much time had passed, and no one would care that much anymore. Besides, both Otis and Eliza were dead. Nothing could help them now.

He shut down the computer and turned out the light in the bedroom he had converted into an office. Working from home had benefits, and he liked having his own business. He'd made a name for himself in this town, known for doing good work at a reasonable price. The Ramsdale house would be a glowing addition to his portfolio, but somehow that didn't seem as important as it once was.

He stepped out onto the deck and looked up at the night sky. With the house lights out behind him, the stars seemed big enough and bright enough to touch. He thought of Allie and wished she wasn't sleeping in the big house by herself. She had the telephone in her room now, but that was only limited protection. He had to find out how someone was getting into that house in spite of the locked doors.

Clay started to go inside when a new thought glimmered at the edge of his mind. He turned around to stare up at the stars as if they had a message for him. He stood very still, letting the idea develop. Of course. There might be a blueprint of the Ramsdale house somewhere. Maybe the public library, or the museum. He'd check them out. There had to be something they were missing. A blueprint might show them where to find it.

He went back inside, locking the door behind him. Tonight his house seemed lonely. He'd never minded being alone before, but that was before he met Allie. She didn't know him very well yet, but he intended to work on that. The better she knew him, the better she would like him. He'd overheard her talking to someone named Howard on the phone that day they'd found the writing on the mirror, and he knew she'd been hurt. He could hear it in her voice. He was willing to give her all the time she needed. Eventually she would learn she could depend on him.

He turned out the light and went to bed, almost asleep before his head hit the pillow.

Allie sat up in bed, startled awake. Taz scrabbled at the door, barking. She eased out of bed, eyes on the door. Had it moved just the barest fraction? She wasn't sure.

Taz was going bonkers, growling and howling like a wolf. She slid her feet into house shoes, thinking frantically of what she could use for a weapon. Nothing. What had she been thinking? Not a blunt instrument in the room.

Taz growled, lunging at the door, hitting it with a thud, then backing off to do the same thing all over again. Give him credit, he had the heart, if not the size. Maybe he could distract whoever was out there long enough for her to do something. Although at the moment she couldn't think of anything she could contribute for their side.

She remembered the insulated cup she had brought upstairs filled with ice water. The thing held a quart of liquid, and she supposed it might be used as a weapon in a pinch. Maybe she could drown the intruder. She giggled, on the verge of hysteria, and caught herself. This wouldn't do. She needed to keep a clear head.

Allie tiptoed across the carpet and eased the door open. The pup lunged toward the opening, and she blocked him with her foot. Her eyes adjusted to the dim glow of the night-light she had left burning in the upper hall. Taz shot past her, snarling. For his size he made a lot of noise.

He was already at the head of the stairs, starting down. Allie stumbled after him. Whatever had upset him must be downstairs. She thought longingly of the telephone in her room. If only she felt free to call someone, but what could she say? My dog is barking? The person who had been invading her home hadn't made any effort to hurt anyone, so surely she would be safe.

Taz lost his balance and tumbled down the last three steps, yelping in surprise. The fall seemed to scare him, because he changed from loyal protector to a scared little puppy hovering close to her feet. She picked him up and cuddled him against her, checking to see if he was all right. He whined a little when she touched his right front leg, but when she put him down, he could still walk on it.

A light glowed in the parlor, spilling out into the foyer. Allie paused, one hand to her throat. Who waited in there? Had her tormentor decided to reveal himself, or herself, tonight? She took a deep breath and started walking. Taz growled and scampered past her toward the dark blue high-backed chair that sat facing away from the door. Suddenly he whirled and scurried back to Allie. She was too frightened to be angry, but someone who had no right to be in her house sat in that chair. Ready or not, it was time for a confrontation.

Allie strode around the chair and dropped the insulated cup she had been gripping all this time. Her mouth opened to scream, but no sound came out. Maude Wheeler sprawled half in and half out of the chair, her face streaked with blood. An ugly gash dented the side of her head. Taz whined. Allie swallowed against the rising tide of bile clogging her throat. Poor Maude. She would never bother anyone again.

After what seemed an eternity when she stood frozen, unable to move, Allie managed to break loose from the stupor that gripped her. She whirled, stumbling up the steps. Clay. She had to call Clay. There was a phone in the parlor, but she couldn't walk past that crumpled, bloody body to reach it. She didn't think of the phone in the kitchen until she was halfway up the stairs. She just knew she had to talk to Clay.

Clay answered on the third ring. The person on the other end of the line was crying so hard, he couldn't tell who it was or what was wrong.

"All right now, calm down. Who is this?"

"Me. It's me, Clay."

"Allie?" He jerked to an upright position. Something was wrong with Allie? "Okay, take a deep breath. Start over, and go slower."

"She's there . . . in the chair."

"Who is where? Allie, help me out here. I can't do anything if I don't know what's wrong."

"Maude Wheeler is dead."

"She's what? How do you know?" And why would she be this upset? There wasn't any love lost between the two of them. Not anything to bring on this hysterical behavior.

"She's dead in my parlor."

That knocked the wind out of him. "She's what?"

"Dead. Here, in the parlor."

"What's she doing there?" At this time of the night? Midnight? "Did she have a heart attack or something?"

"Someone killed her. She's all bloody."

His own blood chilled. "Look, I'm on my way. I'll be there in five minutes. Okay?"

"Clay, hurry."

"I will. Trust me."

Clay pulled on jeans and a sweatshirt, grabbed his car keys, and headed for the door. Someone had killed Maude? And in the Ramsdale house? What was going on here? He drove the short distance, parked in the driveway, and shut off the motor, realizing he dreaded facing what waited for him behind that door. Everyone in Stony Point knew that Maude Wheeler hated Allie McGregor. Now she was dead in Allie's house.

Their intruder had just upped the ante.

Chapter Ten

Allie saw the car lights and met him at the door. "Oh, Clay, it's awful."

He held her close. "It's all right. Don't worry, Allie, we'll face this together."

She looked up at him. "They'll think I did it, won't they?"

He shook his head. "You're innocent. You couldn't hurt anyone. The police will know that."

Allie didn't believe him, but it wouldn't help to say so. She gestured toward the parlor. "In there."

He put her gently aside and walked toward the doorway. "Where's the dog?"

"Shut up in my room." As if on cue, Taz erupted in a frenzy of barking. "I'd better go get him. He'll ruin the door if he keeps on scratching at it like that."

Clay hesitated. "I don't want you going up there by yourself. I'll go with you."

When Allie opened the door, Taz hurtled through, growling a warning. Clay caught him. "What do you think you're doing?"

At the familiar voice the little dog calmed, wiggling and trying to lick Clay's face. They went downstairs together, and Clay walked around to look at Maude. He stood quietly, hands in his pockets, not touching anything, just looking.

Allie waited in the doorway. She couldn't go inside that room again if her life depended on it. In fact, she might never go into that room again. She could close her eyes and see Maude's surprised face. That stopped her. *Surprised?* Surely she was being fanciful. She didn't think dead features held an expression. Probably Maude *had* been surprised, though, because there wasn't any sign of struggle. Someone she trusted must have dealt that fatal blow.

Clay joined her in the doorway. "We have to call the police." She nodded. "Use the kitchen phone."

He turned on the light, and Allie slumped down in a chair, still holding Taz in her arms. He'd struggled to follow Clay into the parlor, but she had refused to put him down.

Clay gave directions to the dispatcher and hung up the phone. "They'll be here in a few minutes. Is there anything you need to tell me?"

She shook her head. "Taz woke me. He was barking and trying to get out of the room. I followed him down here and found her. Who could have done anything so terrible?"

"I don't know. That's for the police to find out. Allie, do you want to call John Bailey?"

"No, I don't. That would seem like an admission of guilt, and I didn't kill her, Clay. I swear I didn't."

The wail of sirens cut the night. He lifted her from the chair, his expression so fierce, it frightened her a little.

"I know you didn't, Allie. I won't let anyone blame you. I promise." He patted her shoulder. "You stay here. I'll let them in."

He left the kitchen, and Allie sank back into the chair and wrapped her arms around Taz. She could hear footsteps and the murmur of voices behind the closed door. Eventually they would come to question her. She stared at the night-darkened windows, seeing the flicker of lights as more vehicles pulled into her drive. Her thoughts flitted in one direction, then another, and she tried to compose herself. She would need a clear, focused mind when talking to the police.

She sat there for some time, just waiting, then slowly got to her feet. The police would probably be here for a while. She washed her hands and started a pot of coffee. A sound came from behind her, and she whirled, one hand pressed against her throat, half expecting to see the police . . . or maybe the murderer. Cora entered, wrapped in an all-weather coat. Allie crumpled in relief.

Cora strode toward her, arms outstretched. "Oh, Allie, I'm so sorry you had to be the one to find her."

"Is she still there?"

"I guess so. They wouldn't let me into the parlor, but the ambulance is here. What happened?"

Allie told the story she knew she'd have to tell over and over. "Oh, Cora, I know she was a very disagreeable woman, but who could have done that to her?"

Cora drew Allie over to the table. "Let's sit down. I'm still weak from the shock. I heard the sirens, of course, and saw the lights, and I was afraid something had happened to you, so I ran over, and Clay met me in the foyer and told me what was going on."

"I guess they woke up the neighborhood," Allie said. "A lovely introduction to the people I haven't met."

"They woke Harry at any rate," Cora said. "He's sitting in the foyer trying to look like he belongs there."

"You don't like Harry, do you?"

Cora looked thoughtful. "I don't know for sure. He just appeared out of nowhere, looking for a job, and in light of the funny stuff going on around here . . ." She hesitated. "Oh, Allie. I'm sorry. I didn't mean Maude's death was funny."

"I know that. It's just . . ."

"Yeah," Cora agreed. "Just plain horrible. Like all of the other things that sort of escalated to this."

"I don't see how Harry could have had anything to do with it. Did he know Maude?"

"That's the problem," Cora said. "We don't know what Harry knows and what he doesn't. He's a stranger, and I'm not in the mood to trust strangers right now."

"Well, I'm sure the police will check him out, just as they will the rest of us."

"And that's another thing I don't like. We're innocent, but we'll be grilled just like any other suspect, and the real murderer probably won't even be questioned."

"You don't know that," Allie protested. "They'll check into Maude's background, find out things we don't know."

Cora sniffed. "Checking her background should be fun. She's run with some far-out characters."

Allie grasped at this very slim straw. "Maybe one of them bashed her in my parlor."

Clay entered the kitchen. "I smell coffee." It was as somber as a wake in there. Both women looked stricken. He could understand that. They'd worked so hard, and now this. Nothing like a murder to shoot down your plans for opening a bed-and-breakfast.

"Help yourself. I thought the police might want some later," Allie said.

"I'm sure they will." Clay poured a cup of the steaming liquid and carried it over to the table. "They're busy right now, but they want to talk to us as soon as they've finished."

Harry peered around the edge of the door. "Okay if I come in? I'm in the way out here."

Clay waved him in and motioned toward the coffeepot. "Cups are on the counter." He noticed Allie's barely suppressed resentment at his making himself so at home and including Harry. Well, tough. He knew she was bound to be sensitive right now, but he wanted to talk to the new maintenance man. He didn't know one thing about this guy, and it was time to ask a few questions. He couldn't overlook the little fact that Maude had been killed after Harry showed up. The man lived on the premises now too. Right handy, so to speak.

Harry sat down at the table, looking ill at ease. "Who got killed?"

"Maude Wheeler. You know her?" Clay watched for his reaction.

Harry shrugged. "Don't think so. What did she do?"

"Ran a bookstore and belonged to one of those cults." And hadn't Harry told him he'd overheard Maude Wheeler talking about Allie's turning the Ramsdale house into a bed-and-breakfast?

"The kind that believes in crystals and rolling stones?"

"I think that's runic stones," Cora said.

"Whatever." Harry waved away the correction. "Never understood how anyone could believe that stuff. Sounds weird to me. Who found her?"

"I did."

Allie sounded exhausted. No wonder. She'd been through a lot tonight, but she was hanging in there. He'd never met a woman as determined as she was proving to be. She was tough—had to give her that.

"I wish I'd been here," Harry said, and Allie blinked at the obvious compassion in his voice. "You didn't need to see anything like that."

"I called Clay."

"Well, now, I guess that was the best thing for you to do." Harry smiled. "He'd come anytime you needed him."

Allie blushed. "I never thought to call you, Harry. I'm sorry."

"You will next time. Clay's someone you can depend on, but I'm just a few steps away." Harry stood up. "Guess I'll see what the police are doing now."

He left, and Cora shook her head. "You know I didn't like Harry at first, but he seems all right. Just takes some getting used to."

Clay silently agreed, but he had a feeling about Harry. On the surface he seemed all right, but something just didn't fit. He couldn't put his finger on it, but Harry would bear watching. Maybe it *was* a good thing he lived on the estate, where Clay could keep an eye on him.

Cora took lunch meat from the refrigerator and opened a loaf of bread. "I'll make some sandwiches. Those men are going to be working for a while. They might appreciate something to eat."

"Good idea," Clay said. "I'll make another pot of coffee." He glanced at Allie. "If that's all right with you."

She waved in a gesture of dismissal. "Whatever. Might as well be nice to them—maybe they'll give me their best cell."

Cora dropped the knife she'd been using to spread mayonnaise. "Oh, Allie. Don't talk like that. They won't arrest you."

"They might. Half of Stony Point knew that Maude and I were having trouble. She was killed in my house, and I found her. The house is locked tight—no way in unless I open the door and let her in."

"That's not true. We've had prowlers here from the day you first arrived."

"The police won't know that."

"We'll tell them." Cora sounded fierce. "Don't worry, we're with you all the way in this."

Clay wanted to agree with Cora, but he knew Allie had a point. The police were sure to suspect her of murdering Maude. Although he knew she was innocent, he couldn't deny that the evidence so far pointed in her direction.

A policeman appeared in the doorway. "Miss McGregor?"

Allie rose. "I'm right here." Now that the time had come, she was relieved to find that her nerves had steadied.

He nodded. "Would you come with me, please?"

Clay started to get up, and the policeman shook his head. "Just Miss McGregor right now. We'll get to the rest of you in time."

Allie motioned toward the food. "There are sandwiches and coffee. Will you tell the others, please?"

He smiled. "I'll do that. It's nice of you to think of us."

She walked out of the kitchen, and he followed, closing the door behind him. "We've taken over your office for the time being. I hope that's all right."

"It's fine." As if she had a choice. It seemed strange to see someone else sitting at her desk while she had to sit across from him.

The man behind the desk smiled at her, but his eyes were watchful. He looked to be in his early thirties, with sandy blond hair cut short and a bushy mustache. "Sergeant Joe Garret, Miss McGregor. Like to ask you some questions."

"Of course." She folded her hands in her lap and waited.

"You knew the deceased?"

"Maude Wheeler. I met her the day I came to inspect this house after learning my aunt had left it to me."

"Could you tell me about that meeting?"

"There isn't much to tell. She just showed up in my parlor, claiming the house should belong to her."

A smile flickered in his eyes. "That sounds like Maude."

"You knew her?" *Please don't let him be one of her best friends.*

"Yeah, I knew her. She had a habit of showing up at city council meetings with an agenda. Some of them were rather strange. Was that the only time you've seen her?"

"No, I stopped by her bookstore one day to look for a book on Painted Ladies."

"Painted Ladies, like in houses?"

"What else? Oh." She smiled. "Houses, not women."

"I guess she was glad to see you."

"No, she wasn't." Allie stopped to think back. "In fact, she practically threw me out of the store."

"That right? Was she in the habit of coming here?"

"She came one other time. Cora Witner and I had just returned from church, and Maude and Mary Olson were sitting on the porch waiting for us. That time she told me she had owned the house in a previous life and so of course it should belong to her."

"I see. I was hoping you might have some insight into who might have killed her."

Allie shook her head. "None."

"Clay seemed to think some strange things had been happening in the house. Care to tell me about them?"

She shrugged. "Just things being moved around, messages written in lipstick on mirrors. Things like that. Music played when no one was there. And a phone call telling me to get out. Oh, yes, someone left a dead rabbit on my bed with plastic flowers arranged around it, like a funeral or something."

"Anyone else know about these things?"

"Yes. Cora Witner noticed them."

He frowned. "Let me get this straight. Things were moved from one place to another, but no one saw them being moved. Just noticed them in a new place."

"That's right."

"Anyone else hear the music, except you?"

"No." She stopped, seeing the danger too late.

"Anyone else get a phone call?"

She shook her head reluctantly.

"So all we have is your word that these things happened."

"You think I'm making it up. Why would I do that?"

"Well, if I was an evil-minded man, which I'm not"—he shook his head, as if denying such a thing—"I might think you were trying to make people think someone else was doing these things. Sort of setting up a hypothetical intruder who just might commit murder."

"Thereby taking myself off the hook." She looked him in the eye. "You think I did it?"

"I'm not sure. But I think it's a possibility."

"I see. In that case, I don't think I'll talk to you anymore."

"It might be in your best interests if you did. Otherwise I might believe you had something to hide. Did you invite Maude Wheeler here tonight?"

"No! Why would I do that? At this hour of the night? Don't be ridiculous."

His lips firmed. "You were alone here. No opportunity for anyone to interrupt you. Doesn't seem ridiculous to me. Did you fight over the house?"

"We didn't fight over anything. Why would I kill her in my own home?"

"Whoever bashed her with a poker hadn't exactly planned it. The evidence has all the earmarks of an impulsive killing. Someone just flew off the handle and let her have it."

"It wasn't me."

Finally he let her go, and she went back to the kitchen feeling ill. Clay looked up as she entered. She took a deep breath. "They think I did it."

Clay was next, and he followed the policeman to the office, trying to control his anger. He had thought they would suspect Allie, so it wasn't that much of a surprise, but he hated the way she had looked, just standing there drooping a little, the strain showing on her face.

Joe Garret looked up when he entered and sat down. "Hi, Clay. You doing okay?"

"I guess so. You making any progress?"

"Depends on what you call 'progress.' Do you mean have I solved Maude Wheeler's murder? No, I haven't. If you mean are we making headway in processing the crime scene, then yes, we are."

"Is Maude still here?"

"No, the body was removed half an hour ago. Now, tell me how you came to be here."

"Allie McGregor called me and said she had found Maude Wheeler murdered in the parlor."

"Did you have any reason to suspect she had killed her instead of finding her the way she said?"

"None. Allie McGregor wouldn't kill anyone. She doesn't have it in her."

"Anyone can kill. You'd be surprised what you see in my line of work."

"Allie had no reason to kill anyone."

"Sure, she did. It may not seem like much of a reason to some people, but then, it only had to seem like a good reason to the murderer. Maude was trying to take the house away from Miss McGregor."

"Maude didn't have the chance of a snowball in August of getting this house."

Garret raised his eyebrows. "You sure about that?"

"Very sure. John Bailey wrote that will, and he knows his business. George Aiken has already tried that and didn't get anywhere. You can be sure that will would stand up in any court in the land."

"Maybe Maude planned to scare Miss McGregor away, force her to sell the house."

"Allie would never have done that. Has she told you about the harassment they've had ever since she moved in?"

Garret nodded. "She told me. I'm not sure I believe her."

"Why not? Do you have any proof to the contrary?"

"No, but did anyone besides her actually see anything? Did you?"

"I saw words written on a mirror. That's definite enough." Clay stopped as he remembered the incident. He'd seen the words after Allie had gone to the parlor to answer the phone. Cora had been in the room immediately before Allie entered it and hadn't seen the message. Not until Allie came to the kitchen and told them it was there.

Garret grinned at him. "I don't know what you've remembered, but you look like you've just bitten into a pickle."

Allie sat in the kitchen while the police questioned Cora. Taz lay curled under her chair, snoozing, apparently having adapted to having a houseful of strangers.

A policeman tapped on the door before entering. She hoped their manners were as good when they came to arrest her. She raised her eyebrows. "Yes?"

"One of the desk drawers is locked. We'd like to have the key."

She got up and went to the office, too tired to be angry. "The key is in the shallow drawer in the middle."

Joe Garret slid the drawer open, and she indicated the correct key. "You'll find an expanding file given to me by Anna Milcrest. My great-aunt Eliza Ramsdale gave it to Anna to keep for me. It has all of the information she collected pertaining to her husband, Otis Ramsdale's, arrest and imprisonment."

Garrett opened the drawer and looked inside the file. "Why did she give you this?"

"She wanted me to try to clear his name. There's a letter from her with the other papers. Apparently she never stopped believing he was innocent."

"I see." He leafed through the file.

"I'd like to have that back. After all this time I realize it would be useless to expect to learn the truth, but I have an obligation to try."

He gave her a searching glance before nodding. "We'll have to look through it, of course, but I can't see how it could have any bearing on the case. I'll make sure it's returned to you."

"Thank you. I appreciate it." She started to leave the room, then turned back. "You'll find sandwiches and coffee for you and your men in the kitchen."

He nodded thanks.

Cora stood in the doorway. "Are you through with us, Joe? If so, I'm taking Allie over to the guesthouse so she can get some rest. We'll both be here tomorrow if you still need to talk to us."

"Fine with me. We'll probably want to follow up, but I guess that's all for tonight."

They crossed the lawn to the guesthouse, Allie carrying Taz. The pup lifted his nose to sniff the night air. The moon had almost completed its journey across the sky. The cold dew drenched their shoes, and Allie shivered. She had been so proud of her house. Now it had been tainted by murder.

When they reached the guesthouse, Cora brought out sheets and blankets and made a bed on the couch. "That's a comfortable place to sleep. I should know. I've spent many a night on it when my father was ill. You need to get some rest."

Allie sat down in a chair and leaned her head back. "Oh, Cora. I don't know what to do."

"You can't do anything tonight. Tomorrow will be soon enough to take action."

Dinah stalked into the room. Taz took one look and drooped, head down, expression woebegone. Dinah sat down in the middle of the parlor and cast a cold eye on the occupants. Then she got up and deliberately paced across the floor toward Taz. She stopped in front of him and gently butted him with her head. Taz relaxed a bit and gave a tentative wag of his tail. Dinah rubbed her head against him, and the puppy slumped to the floor. The cat collapsed beside him, her head resting on the dog's back.

"Well, would you look at that," Cora said. "I've always heard that the day will come when the lion shall lie down with the lamb, but I don't remember anything about dogs and cats."

Chapter Eleven

Allie gasped for air. A hundred-pound weight crushed her chest. She couldn't breath. *Heart attack!* A rumble like a runaway freight train brought her fully awake. A gray and white furry, triangular face hovered in her line of vision. Green eyes narrowed to slits peered at her as if considering the advisability of attacking. *Dinah!*

"You . . . cat! Get off me."

Dinah rose, stretched, kneaded Allie's chest with her front feet, then, with a contemptuous air, jumped to the floor. Taz pranced sideways to meet her, his rear almost even with his head, tail wagging. Dinah allowed him to swipe one of her ears with her tongue before jumping into a chair and stretching out in royal comfort. Taz reared up on his hind legs, uttering timid little puppy barks, tail whipping back and forth like a semaphore in a hurricane.

Allie sighed. Even her dog had deserted her. She threw back the blanket and sat up, the events of the night rushing back to assault her. Maude. The blood. The police. She swung her feet to the floor, jarred into action. Would the police show up to arrest her today? If so, she needed to be up and fully dressed, not bleary-eyed with sleep and wearing Cora's nightgown and having bed head.

She folded her bedding and stacked it neatly on one end of the couch. Cora entered from the kitchen. "I didn't know you were up. Did I wake you?"

"No, Dinah did." Allie stretched and yawned. "I feel like I've been asleep for a hundred years."

"A modern-day Rip Van Winkle? I feel sluggish myself. I'll get you a toothbrush, and you can clean up as best you can before breakfast."

"I feel homeless. No clean clothes. When do you think they'll let me go back home?"

"Sometime today, surely. They were over there all night. I heard the cars leaving somewhere between four and five this morning."

"I can't believe someone killed Maude Wheeler in my parlor." Allie walked over to the window and looked out at her house. It gleamed, as if it were brand-spanking-new, with a fresh coat of paint and the neat beds of perennials and annuals Harry had planted and tended with such care.

Taz barked at Dinah, and Allie turned from the window. "I'll freshen up and be right with you."

"No hurry. We're just having bacon and scrambled eggs and toast. I'm not in the mood to get fancy this morning."

Allie eyed her reflection in the bathroom mirror and considered that Cora might have a point. *Fancy* didn't approach the way she looked. Bags, big as overnight cases, puffed under her eyes. Her complexion looked grimy, although she had washed last night. Worse of all, her anxious expression made it appear as if she expected to be arrested at any time. Well, to tell the truth, she did feel that way, but it might help if she didn't look so guilty.

She washed her face and slathered on lily-of-the-valley lotion, which she had bought for Cora. The toothpaste brand was different from what she used, but it would do. This was no time to be picky. There wasn't much she could do to her hair except brush it back from her face. How could she have come to look so tacky overnight? If worry did this to her, she'd be a hag when she came out of prison.

They ate breakfast and lingered over cups of fragrant coffee. Cora slipped Taz a crust of toast, and Allie raised her eyebrows. "You're feeding a dog?"

Cora shrugged. "He grows on one."

"That he does. I suppose Dinah would in time if I could

keep her from sleeping on my chest. I woke up dying from lack of air."

"She did that to me the other night. I've started shutting her out of my bedroom."

"So she shared mine."

"Allie? What are you going to do now?"

"I don't know. Wait until the police make a move, I guess. Oh, Cora, I've just begun to realize how much I want this bed-and-breakfast. I've never done anything before that amounted to much."

"We'll have our bed-and-breakfast. Nothing is going to stop us. We've invested too much to give up."

"What if they arrest me?"

"They won't. Joe Garret has too much sense to suspect you."

"You know better than that, but thanks for trying to make me feel better. I'm the only suspect right now."

Cora fiddled with a teaspoon. "We have to find out how someone is getting into the house. There has to be something we're missing."

"I don't know what it could be. I've thought until my brain is numb, and I can't come up with anything."

"Don't you give up. We're going to find out who killed Maude. We won't stop until we do."

" 'We'?"

Cora blinked back the tears swimming in her eyes. "You were there when I needed help. Do you think I'd desert you now? We're in this together."

Allie wiped her own eyes. "I don't deserve you."

Cora shook her head and attempted a smile, which fell short. "Where would I go if something happened to you? I couldn't move in with Blakely. Not after I've had a taste of freedom."

The phone rang, and she answered, listened for a minute, and then handed the receiver to Allie. "It's for you."

Clay was on the other end. "The police are finished, and they said it was okay for you to come back anytime."

"We'll be right there. Are you at the house?"

"No, I'm in my car, on my way to pick up some grout for the bathroom tile. I'll be there as soon as I can."

Allie finished the call and handed the receiver to Cora. "We can go back. Unless you have things to do this morning."

"Nothing that can't wait. I'm going with you."

They left Taz and Dinah behind and crossed the yard to the house. Cora used her key to unlock the front door, and they went directly to the parlor. Black fingerprint powder covered everything. The chair where Maude had sat was gone. The fireplace poker was missing, along with an area rug.

Allie stopped inside the door. "I thought I'd always remember her there, but I don't. It's as if she didn't exist."

"She existed, all right, and she did what she could to cause trouble. It got her killed. We don't know the why of it yet, but we will. I'll get a broom and dustpan and get started cleaning."

"I'll help." Maybe cleaning the room would cleanse her mind of the memories.

They had finished the parlor and were ready to move on to the office when the doorbell rang. Cora opened the door to find Mary Olson. For a minute Allie thought she might close the door in the woman's face, but then she relented and allowed her to come in.

Mary looked less like a mouse today. Maude's death seemed to have infused her with a shot of courage. She stepped inside, head high and eyes direct. "You didn't want to let me in. I have a right to be here."

"Now, don't you start that spirit malarkey," Cora said, her tone on the peevish side. "We've had enough of that to last for a while."

Mary stood her ground. "I had to hear from my next-door neighbor that Maude was dead. You could have called me."

"We were a little busy with the police and all, and, besides, I'm not aware we have your number. Are you in the book?"

"As a matter of fact I am. I'm here because I want to see where my best friend died."

Cora sighed. "Look, Mary. Let's start over. I'm sorry I was snippy, but I've just about reached the end of my rope, what with one thing and another. It won't do you any good to see because there's nothing left to see. The police took everything."

"Just the same, I have a right to know."

"We can't tell you what happened, Mary, because we don't know ourselves." Allie motioned toward the parlor. "However, you're welcome to come in."

"I know what happened," Mary said. "Maude made the spirits angry when she insisted the house belonged to her. It didn't, and I tried to tell her so, but she wouldn't listen."

"A spirit didn't hit Maude in the head with a poker," Cora said, her voice as tart as a newly sliced lemon.

Mary ignored her. "It's a pity Maude had to die, but at least you won't be opening a bed-and-breakfast now."

"Of course we will," Allie protested. "It might put off the opening date, but we're aren't beat yet." She realized that also depended on the police and what they decided to do, but she didn't feel inclined to discuss that with Mary.

Mary smirked. "No one will come now."

Cora glared at her. "That's not true."

"Otis Ramsdale's house should not be turned into a commercial enterprise. He was one of the leading men in Stony Point in his time."

"Oh, is that so?" Cora bristled, her impatience turning to obvious anger. "A bed-and-breakfast is a respectable business."

Mary smiled. "You don't own the house."

"Neither do you. Therefore, it's not for you to say how the house should be used."

Allie decided to try to defuse the situation. "I do own the house, and we plan to open by the end of June."

Mary's expression glowed with satisfaction. "If you're not in jail."

"There is that," Allie conceded.

Mary's eyes glittered with what looked like anger. "Eliza

should never have left you the house in the first place. All she did was cause trouble."

Clay wandered the aisles of the hardware store, supposedly picking up paint samples so Allie and Cora could choose colors for the new bathroom. His mind churned with questions about last night's tragedy. He had a suspicion Allie was in danger, but he didn't have any real reason for feeling that way.

He turned the corner and met Roger Axelrod. Something in the other man's face said the meeting wasn't all that accidental.

"Hey, Roger. How's it going?"

"All right, I guess." Roger hesitated. "I hear there was trouble out at the Ramsdale house last night."

"Yeah," Clay admitted. "Someone killed Maude Wheeler."

Roger nodded. "That's what I heard. Cora doing all right?"

"She was the last time I talked to her."

Roger looked worried. "I knew Maude. Well, you did too. It's a miracle someone didn't murder her long ago." He looked ashamed. "I guess I shouldn't have said that."

Clay grinned. "I know what you mean. Maude had gotten so rigid in her thinking, she didn't leave room for anyone else to have an opinion."

"I wouldn't be surprised if that was what got her killed."

Clay realized he felt the same way, he just hadn't admitted it. At least, not out loud. "I'm going to the Ramsdale house. Why don't you come along?"

"Oh, I guess I probably shouldn't. Wouldn't want to be in the way."

"We've done a lot of work on the house. Wouldn't you like to see it?"

Roger brightened. "I guess everyone in town would like to see the inside of Miss Eliza's house, especially now that it's been restored. If you think it will be all right."

From his expression, Clay realized Roger really wanted to see Cora, and that was just fine. He wanted to check on Allie again. Last night had been a rough experience for her. Well, it had been rough on all of them. A police investigation wasn't anything to look forward to. He just wanted to let her know he was there if she needed him. Funny, he went into this just wanting to get a job. Now he was emotionally bound up with the woman who owned the house. He'd always been careful not to overstep the professional line between him and the client. The way he was beginning to feel about Allie McGregor had taken him by surprise, but he was going to find out what was going on before she got hurt. And that was a promise. Now he hastened to reassure Roger.

"It'll be just fine, and I know Cora and Allie will appreciate your coming. They need friends right now."

Mary was still at the house, and Allie was about to pull her hair in frustration. She'd never in her life seen anyone who could get in the way more and do less. Clay's truck pulled into the drive and stopped.

Cora looked out the window. "Oh, good, Roger is with him. He'll know what to do."

Allie grinned. *Wasn't love grand?* You just had to look at Cora to see she was happy and relieved to see Roger. She realized that wasn't so funny after all, considering how relieved she was to see Clay.

Mary got up from her chair. "Roger who?"

"Roger Axelrod. He's an old friend," Cora said absently, intent on the two men climbing the porch steps. She hurried to open the door.

Mary hesitated, looking conflicted; then, to Allie's amazement, she shoved her way past Cora, pushed past the two men, and strode across the porch and down the steps.

Cora jerked around to stare after her. "Well, what lit her fire?"

"I guess she didn't want company," Allie said. "How nice of you to come, Roger. We appreciate it."

He flushed. "Clay invited me over to see the house."

Cora raised her eyebrows. "And here we thought you came to see us."

Roger grinned. "Actually, I did. The house was just an excuse."

"Now, that's more like it." Cora indicated the wicker chairs. "It's so nice today, let's sit out here. I've got a pitcher of lemon herbal drink I'm experimenting with. I'll bring it out, and we'll just relax."

"I can't think of anything I'd like better," Clay said. "After last night, I need to relax."

Allie brought out the lemon drink while Cora ran a plate of cheese and mushroom snacks under the broiler for a few minutes. They sat on the wide front porch, enjoying the spring day and talking about the murder. Allie wished they could find another subject, but she knew it was uppermost in their minds.

Clay ran a finger down the beaded moisture on his glass. "I know you'll probably not like to hear this, Allie, but I don't want you staying here alone at night. I'm not sure it's safe."

"I'm not happy about it either, but I refuse to leave. This is my home, and I don't plan to let anyone run me out, no matter what they do."

"I wish you'd stay at the guesthouse with me," Cora said. "Or I could sleep over here until we get this straightened out."

"I'll be all right. Nothing has bothered me so far."

There was always a first time, Clay thought, but he didn't want to make it any harder for her than it already was.

"When do you plan to open your inn?" Roger asked.

"As soon as we can," Allie replied. "I guess we need to advertise somewhere, but I don't know exactly how to go about it."

Roger looked thoughtful. "Have you listed it with a reservation service agency?"

"Actually, I've never heard of one. What do they do?"

"Advertise your business and handle bookings. I can get you the name of a couple if you'd like."

"Oh, we'd like," Cora said. "We need all the help we can get. We're sort of feeling our way on this."

"We can fix up the place and make it attractive to people, and Cora has a fabulous breakfast menu planned, but unless we get customers, none of it matters, so any information you can give us will surely be appreciated." Allie took the last cheese snack. "I love these. New recipe?"

"Something I experimented with," Cora said. "I'm thinking of trying focaccia bread next."

"Sounds good," Roger said. "If you need a taster, I'm available."

Clay set his glass on the table. "Allie, I'd like for you to inspect the new herb beds Harry is putting in. He wants to make an herb garden at the back of the carriage house where it will be out of the way but still be handy to the kitchen."

Allie blinked at the sudden turn of conversation, but she got to her feet. "I don't know much about horticulture. He's doing such a good job, I don't want to upset him by making suggestions."

"You're the owner. You need to know what's being done on your property," Clay insisted. "Come on, a walk in the fresh air will do you good. I'll bet you haven't been out much today."

Clay figured Roger would like some time alone with Cora. He led Allie around the side of the house. She looked up at him, and he took her hand in his, swinging it gently. He didn't care a rap about Harry's herb garden. He just wanted some time alone with Allie. Wanted to do something to take that worried expression off her face.

The herb garden, when they reached it, was a welcome diversion. Harry had cleared a space in back of the carriage house and had dug the garden in the shape of a wagon wheel. In the center he'd planted lemon-gem marigold, their dainty yellow blooms creating a bright hub to the wheel. The rest of the bed was separated into pie-shaped segments filled with fragrant herbs.

Allie stopped to brush her hand against a rosemary bush. The soft, piney fragrance filled the air. "Rosemary for remembrance," she murmured.

Clay plucked a stem of tarragon, savoring the licorice-laden scent. "I don't know what half of these are."

"I don't know either," Allie admitted. "I'll bet Cora does, though."

"Probably so. Cora's a smart woman."

"She's a wonderful woman, and I hope Roger has sense enough to see it."

"I think Roger knows exactly what she's like, and unless I miss my guess, he's not planning to let her get away from him."

"I don't know what I'd do without her, but she has a right to a home and life of her own."

"What about you, Allie? What do you want?"

"What every woman wants, I suppose." She kept her face turned from him. He pulled her around to where he could meet her eyes. Tears ran down her cheeks. "Oh, Clay. I'm scared. What if they arrest me?"

He draped an arm around her shoulders. "They won't. We're going to find the guilty person—I promise you that. I won't let them hurt you."

Now all he had to do was keep that promise. One thing for sure, he would do everything in his power to keep her safe. She didn't deserve what someone was trying to do to her. They strolled back to the front of the house. The glasses and dishes from their snack had been cleared away, but Roger's car was still there, so Clay supposed he'd walked back to the guesthouse with Cora.

Allie looked up at the looming presence of the Queen Anne mansion. "I'm so proud of this house and what we've accomplished. It's the first thing I've done without my parents giving advice, and it's beautiful, isn't it?"

"Yes, it is," Clay agreed. "And it's going to be a successful bed-and-breakfast, just wait and see. It'll come out all right in the end. Give it time."

"I hope I have time." Allie climbed the steps.

Clay stood beside her, admitting to himself how hard it was to leave. She wouldn't hear of his staying, though; he knew her too well already to even suggest it. He brushed a lock of hair away from her cheek. "I have to go now—things I need to do—but I'll call you later to see if you're all right, and you have my number. If anything bothers you, anything at all, you call, and I'll be here."

She smiled. "I will."

He drew her close and kissed her lightly, then let her go, watching as she opened the door and stepped inside. She paused and looked back. "Clay . . . thank you."

"Hey, no problem. That's my life mission, rescuing damsels in distress."

She laughed and closed the door behind her. He walked out to his pickup to find Harry leaning against the driver's side. The older man straightened up. "Afternoon."

Clay nodded. "Everything all right?"

"So far," Harry said. "I just wanted to tell you I'll be watching tonight. If anyone comes around, I'll know."

"Let me give you my number. If anything happens, you call."

"I'll do that." Harry took the scrap of paper. He looked up at the tower room, where a light had come on. "She's a good one, like Eliza."

"You knew Eliza?" Clay asked.

"A lot of people knew Eliza," Harry said. "I'll see you around."

Clay watched him walk back to the carriage house, wondering how Harry Dalton could have been acquainted with Eliza Ramsdale.

Chapter Twelve

Allie got ready for bed but was too restless to settle down. The events of the night before haunted her. Maude had been killed while she slept upstairs. Only Taz's barking had alerted her. She paced to the window, looking out but seeing nothing except the sleeping garden and a full moon drifting through clouds laced with gray and silver.

Taz stayed close beside her, body trembling as if cold. Or afraid? Had he sensed something disturbing, or had he picked up on her own anxiety? She scooped him up in her arms, and he snuggled close, his tail giving a tentative wag. Allie smiled, thinking he was comforted by her presence just the way she felt comforted by having him in her room. She gently placed the pup on the foot of the bed. He opened one eye, and she scratched his ears.

"Don't get used to sleeping here. It's just a one-time thing." A little reward for how he had tried to protect her last night. Finding him had been one of life's blessings, as far as she was concerned. He was company, and he never questioned or doubted her. Just gave his unqualified love and trust.

She turned out the light and slept peacefully until morning. The night passed without any notice of an unwanted visitor, but when she went downstairs, a table light had been turned on in the parlor.

Allie was working in one of the second-floor bedrooms when Sergeant Joe Garret and Deputy Roy Hastert arrived, both men in uniform and driving a police car. Cora had run upstairs to tell Allie they were there, and Clay and Harry, who were installing cabinets in the third-floor bathroom, heard her and came down to join them.

Joe nodded when they came in. The two men's very attitude stated "official business." "We'd like to ask you a few more questions."

Allie flushed and bit her lip. "I've told you everything I know."

"Humor me. Sometimes we forget important details. You might come up with something we missed the other night."

Clay touched her shoulder, and she glanced up at him, looking startled. "Go along with them. They're just trying to find out the truth."

Her expression showed that she wanted to disagree, but eventually she shrugged and sat down, hands clasping the chair arms. Clay, Cora, and Harry found seats and waited. Clay noticed absently that Harry looked almost as nervous as Allie.

Garret took a small notebook out of his pocket. "Now, let's see. According to this, you never heard anything until the dog barked. That right?"

Allie nodded.

"Okay, now Roy here is going to go up to your room, and we're going to put on a little skit, and he's going to tell us what he hears."

"I assume he won't be asleep." Allie didn't try to hide the sarcasm in her voice, and Clay suppressed a grin. She was a fighter, all right.

"We'll take that into consideration," Garret said. "Point taken."

Roy left the room, and Clay went with him to see that he was actually in Allie's room with the door closed. He also wanted to make sure nothing was hidden there to be discovered later. Not that he really thought Roy or Joe would do that. He'd known them for years, but he didn't feel like taking chances where Allie was concerned.

*   *   *

Downstairs Joe Garret directed his skit. "Now, Harry, I want you to talk to Cora—not really loud, just in a conversational voice."

"What d'you want us to talk about?" Harry asked.

"I don't care, the weather or something. The important thing is to get the sound of voices."

"Gotcha." Harry turned to Cora. "Nice weather we're having, isn't it?"

Cora rolled her eyes. "This is ridiculous."

"Maybe so," Garret said, a note of exasperation in his voice. "Just go along with it, please."

"All right." Cora turned to Harry. "Reckon the rain will warp the rhubarb?"

"Very funny." Garret grinned. "Now talk a little louder, like you're both hard of hearing, and sound like you're upset at something."

"Don't mouth off." Harry jacked up the volume. "Think you're smart?"

"I am smart. You want to make something of it?" Cora responded, her voice at a louder decibel than Allie had ever heard. Cora never raised her voice. She didn't have to. One look and you knew what she had in mind.

"Good, good." Garret nodded. "Now, Harry, you pick up that fireplace shovel and hit the cushioned back of that chair."

It wasn't the chair Maude had been sitting in, of course, but the sound was realistic enough when Harry swung the shovel and smacked the upholstery. Allie winced at the noise of the impact. Just the same, she made a note to remind Chief Garret to give back her poker. The fireplace tools were a matched set that had come with the house. She'd never be able to look at the poker without remembering the use to which it had been put, but it belonged here, and she wanted it back.

The police chief walked to the foot of the stairs and called up to Roy. "Did you hear that?"

The door to Allie's bedroom opened, and Roy peered out. "Did you call?"

"Yes. Did you hear anything?"

"Nothing until I heard you yell. These old houses were built so well, they're almost soundproof. Not like the modern stuff we get today."

Garret ignored this. "Come on down here. I guess we're finished with that for now."

The two men joined the others in the library. Roy shook his head. "We couldn't hear anything, and if she had been asleep like she claimed . . . well, not much chance of hearing a fight, even."

"Okay, now if it's all right with you, we'd like to look for another way into this house. Either someone has a key, or there's something we're overlooking."

"Go ahead," Allie said. "I'd like that little mystery cleared up myself. But we've looked. If there is another door, it won't be easy to find. I wish I could have gotten my hands on the blueprints."

"Well, we've got to try," Garret said. "You go on about your business. We'll do our best not to get in your way."

"Harry and I will help," Clay said.

Garret shot him a look and apparently decided he wasn't going to give in. "All right, but *you* don't get in *our* way."

The men left to look outside first, and Cora and Allie went back upstairs, although they had a hard time concentrating on decorating details with a search party going on outside.

"You think they'll find anything?" Cora asked.

"I don't know. If there's another way in, it seems we'd have found it before now."

"Yes, I know, but there has to be a hidden entrance somewhere." Cora looked frustrated. "We know someone is getting in."

"Well, if it's there, maybe they'll find it." Allie resigned herself to the inevitable. "I doubt if they will, though. Clay's already looked."

"At least they know you couldn't have heard anything going on down here that night." Cora moved a basket of silk flowers to another spot on the goodies table. "That's in your favor."

"Not if they don't find that entrance, it isn't," Allie said. "They'll just claim I killed her, so it wouldn't matter if I could hear upstairs or not, since presumably I'd be down there bopping Maude on the head."

Clay and Harry let the two policemen lead the way around the house. The basement only had small windows with window wells, and from the accumulated dirt and cobwebs over the panes, they obviously hadn't been used for a clandestine entry. One broken window had a few short gray hairs caught on the jagged glass. Probably how Dinah had gotten in the house. Harry brought pruning shears and obligingly chopped at an overgrown forsythia bush Roy thought might be covering an extra window. They ended up with a mutilated bush and a blank wall.

Joe Garret kicked a rock out of his way, probably the closest he would allow himself to come to a temper fit. "All right, Clay. I've given your theory a chance, but I'd like for you to show me how anyone could have gotten inside this house while it was locked up tighter than a miser's piggy bank."

Clay's throat tightened. He had to direct their attention away from Allie. "Maybe he has a key."

"The locks have been changed recently, in case you've forgotten."

"That doesn't mean someone hasn't managed to get a key. Several people have an interest in this house."

"Like who?"

"George and Renata Aiken for example, and that bunch Maude belonged to. Any of them could have managed to get a key and try to scare Allie into selling."

"Fine. Now explain why any of them would kill Maude Wheeler."

"Explain why Allie would."

"Maude was harassing her on the subject of this house."

"You think killing her was the only way to cope?" Clay knew he was pushing it, but he couldn't let Allie down. If there was any way possible, he had to give the police a new lead. Joe Garret was fair, and Clay knew him well enough to be sure he only wanted the truth. But he had to admit, it looked bad for Allie.

Harry gathered the pruned forsythia branches and piled them off to the side. "I don't think Allie and Cora would lie about the strange things going on around here. Why would they? And I'm betting neither would have what it takes to kill someone. They're not that cold-blooded."

Joe narrowed his eyes, considering. "You have anyone else in mind?"

Harry shook his head. "Wish I did, but I'm keeping my eyes open. There's something rotten here. Stinks to high heaven, and I'm betting it isn't over yet."

Clay's blood chilled. He had a feeling Harry was right, and Allie was smack-dab in the middle of it. He wished she would agree to move in with Cora, but she was too stubborn to run. *Bullheaded* was the right word.

Garret sighed. "Let's go inside and check out the basement. I'll go as far as I can with you."

"You don't have the evidence to tie Allie to this murder, and you know it," Clay said. "If you did, you wouldn't be here trying to find that door."

Garret twitched his shoulders in what was almost a shrug. "Okay, maybe I don't, but I don't have any evidence that will clear her either."

"You don't have anything, period. Admit it."

"All right, Clay, I don't have anything yet. But I will, and if it points to your lady friend, I'll have no choice except to arrest her. You got that?"

"I guess so." Yes, he had it. But he hadn't given up yet. He followed them inside, surprised to see Harry tagging along. Maybe he had been wrong about the guy. He seemed to be doing what he could to help.

Two hours later the police gave up, and even Clay had to admit, if there was a door, it sure wasn't going to be easily found. So that left someone with a key. He'd find out from

Allie the name of the company that had installed the new locks. Maybe they would have some answers.

Cora had lunch ready, and Allie invited Clay to eat with them. Harry took all of his meals in the house and seemed to enjoy the home cooking and conversation. Today was Mexican: chicken enchiladas, tacos, and burritos. Allie helped put the food onto the table, and Harry filled his plate.

"What a feed, Cora. If you weren't so young, I'd ask you to marry me."

"Get along with you. I'm not all that young."

"You mean you're available?" Harry asked. "I thought Roger had the inside track there."

Cora blushed. "I keep telling everyone we're just friends."

"That's a good basis for a marriage," Harry said. "Pick someone you like. Then when that first glow of romance fades, you won't find that that's all there was."

"That's very sensible," Allie said. "I think you've got something there."

"Yeah, but it won't sell," Harry said. "Trying to mix romance and common sense is about like trying to mix gas and a lighted match, and with about the same results."

The front doorbell rang, and Allie started to push her chair back, but Cora waved a dismissive hand. "I'm up. I'll get it."

She left, and angry voices erupted in the foyer. Rapid footsteps headed their way, and Allie looked up, startled, just in time to see the kitchen door closing behind Harry.

George and Renata Aiken entered the kitchen, followed by an obviously angry Cora. "They pushed right past me. Didn't even bother to say hello. Just walked in like they owned the house."

"What a perceptive observation, darling," Renata cooed. She glanced around the kitchen. "I love what you've done so far, but I'll want to add some touches of my own. Something not quite so bourgeoisie."

Allie got to her feet. "What are you people doing here? Don't you ever give up?"

George's lips turned up in what she supposed was a smile,

but if so, he needed practice. "We've come to offer to settle out of court."

" 'Settle'?" Allie echoed, feeling stupid. In the wake of everything else that had happened, she'd forgotten about the lawsuit. "See my lawyer."

"We don't need to pay a lawyer to take care of something we can handle ourselves," George said. "I'll make you a fair deal. I'll take the house and give you two hundred thousand dollars, and we'll call it even."

"That's a lot of money," Allie said.

"Not for a house like this on a lot this size in Stony Point," Cora said. "That's not counting the money she's already spent on restoration."

Allie smiled at Cora. "It doesn't matter. The house is not for sale. We're going to open a bed-and-breakfast."

Renata glanced at the curtains. "I'll want to change those to something not quite so provincial. I'm not into country."

Allie felt the blood rushing to her face. "I'm so sorry about your hearing problems. I guess I need to talk louder. The house is not for sale, and I'm sorry you don't like my curtains, but that isn't important, since you won't be coming back. Have you talked to John Bailey? He's sure the will he prepared can stand up in court."

George sneered. "You won't be able to operate a bed-and-breakfast if you're in prison for killing Maude Wheeler. The two hundred thousand would pay your lawyer."

"How I pay my lawyer is my business," Allie said, drawing up as much dignity as she could muster. "Now I think it's time for you to leave, and since you won't be leaving anything be-hind, you won't have a reason to come back."

"You can't throw me out of my great-uncle Otis' house," Re-nata said. "I have a right to be here."

"Your great-uncle Otis is dead, and you have no rights here," Allie sputtered. "Leave, now."

Clay got up from the table and stood beside her. "I think the lady said to go. It might be a good idea to respect her wishes. Otherwise I'll have to throw you out."

Cora took off her apron and moved to stand protectively in front of Allie. "I'll help."

George flushed brick red, his lips tightened, and his eyes narrowed to slits. "You don't know who you're dealing with. I don't lose."

"You lost this round," Clay informed him, and Allie thrilled at the underlying current of steel in his voice. "I'll follow you to the door."

George and Renata wheeled and strode out, with Clay right behind them. Allie gripped the back of the chair, thankful for friends like these two. But their steadfast support might not be enough to keep her out of jail.

Anna Milcrest called and asked if it would be all right if she came to see the changes Allie had made in the house.

"Sure, Anna. Do you want me to come get you?"

"No, Kady will bring me. She has some errands to run, and she'll pick me up after about an hour. I think that will be long enough to bother you."

"You're no bother, and I'd be delighted to have you come. I'll be waiting for you on the porch."

Thirty minutes later a bright red convertible pulled in, and Kady got out of the driver's side and hurried around to help Anna. Allie ran down to meet them, and the two of them guided the older woman up the steps, where she sank down in one of the wicker chairs.

"Go along now. I'll be fine." She waved her hand at her granddaughter. "I just want to sit here for a while. It's like old times, and you've fixed it just the way Eliza used to have it."

Allie glanced at her, surprised. "Really? There was only the porch swing when I took over. Clay found the wicker furniture stored in the carriage house."

Anna nodded. "She reached the place where she just didn't care, and she didn't encourage company. I think she spent most of her days behind those doors, not seeing anyone. It just about killed her when Otis died."

Allie didn't want to go over that again. She got to her feet.

"Would you like to see inside? We've done a lot of painting and cleaning."

"Of course, that's why I'm here." Anna took Allie's arm, leaning on her as they walked into the foyer. "Oh, my, it's so nice, and you've left Mercury on the marble-topped table. Eliza loved that statue. Otis bought it for her in Italy and had it shipped home."

"We've left the foyer mostly as it was except for removing a couple of pictures and replacing them with something more compatible."

"I noticed *Washington Crossing the Delaware* is gone and that awful *Stag at Evening*. Otis chose those pictures, and Eliza hated them, but after he was arrested, she wouldn't change a thing he'd done. She wanted it to be the same when he came home."

"Anna, I'd like to talk to you about Otis' family," Allie began, but Anna patted her arm.

"We'll talk about a lot of things, but first show me the lower floor. I'll not try to climb the stairs. But tell me, which room is yours?"

"I took the tower room."

Anna smiled and shook her head. "I can't believe this. That's the room Eliza loved above all others. It's like she's still here. I truly believe she is influencing you. The minute I walked in, I could feel her presence, just the way it used to be."

Allie felt her features freeze. She hadn't expected this of Anna, a dedicated church member. Her expression must have given her away, because Anna laughed.

"I know what you're thinking, and no, I don't mean Eliza's ghost. I only meant you're related to her, and her traits show up in you."

"You think she influences me?" She had enough trouble living in this house where things were moved around on a regular basis and where a woman had been murdered. The last thing she needed was having someone saying that Eliza Ramsdale's spirit was influencing her.

"Well, yes, I did say that, but I didn't mean it the way it sounded. Let me put it another way. You're living in her house, trying to learn more about her, and she left you a commission. I just intended to suggest that you are influenced by all of that, not by her actual presence."

"But you implied that you felt her presence."

"I do. The house looks the way she would have wanted it to look. I know how much she loved this place, and I do almost expect her to come in smiling and reaching out to hug me the way she used to. We had so many good times here, and those memories linger in my mind. I'm not into spiritualism, and I'm sorry if it sounded that way."

"It's just that after Maude, I'm a little skittish. She made claims concerning the house, and I don't want to get into that again."

Anna sat down on the couch and patted the seat beside her. "Sit down, and let's talk about those things you want to know. Maude was a very distant relative to Otis Ramsdale. So distant, he barely acknowledged it. She latched on to that as a reason she should have this house."

Allie's mouth dropped open. "Maude was a relative?"

"Actually, Maude belonged to one of the better branches of Otis' family tree. Most of the family didn't amount to much."

"Eliza left me a letter in that file claiming she thought James Ramsdale might have been the one to steal the jewels and put the blame onto Otis."

Anna pursed her lips, looking thoughtful. "I certainly wouldn't put it past him. James was the family black sheep. He tried to shine up to Eliza, but she wouldn't have anything to do with him."

"Where is he now?" Allie asked.

Anna shrugged. "I have no idea. I seem to remember hearing a rumor that he died, but I'm not sure about that. I do know he was a nasty piece of business, and you shouldn't have anything to do with him."

"If I take on Eliza's request, I have to make some effort to find him."

"Well, if you'll take my advice, you'll get John Bailey to check into it. Anyway, if James is still alive, he'd be older than me, and I'm older than dirt. I don't see what you expect to gain from finding him."

Allie laughed and patted her hand. "If he's as alert and with it as you, he could tell me a lot, if he wanted to."

Anna preened. "I *am* rather well preserved, don't you think?"

"I certainly do, and you're a darling. Would you like some lemonade or iced tea? We usually have one or the other made up in the refrigerator."

"Either one would be nice. Could we have it in here? I'm just enjoying looking at Eliza's house and thinking how much she would have loved what you've done with it."

Allie took a pitcher of tea out of the refrigerator and poured two glasses. Cora had prepared a plate of cookies and tea cakes. Allie added them to the tray and carried it to the parlor, the ice cubes making a tinkling music as she walked.

Anna was standing in front of the mantel, looking at the gold-framed mirror. "I wonder what happened to Eliza's portrait that used to hang there."

Allie set the tray down on the coffee table. "I don't know. In all of our digging through the house, we've never found it."

"That mirror used to hang in the foyer right above the parquet table. You have a picture hanging there now."

She sat back down on the couch, and Allie handed her a glass of tea and a small plate filled with a selection of goodies. Anna sighed in pleasure. "Oh, good. I get to spoil my dinner."

Allie straightened. "Oh, I never thought . . . Don't eat them if you'd rather not."

"And let Cora's good cooking go to waste? Don't be silly. I can always say you forced them on me." Anna bit into a tea cake with a blissful expression. "You have no idea how tired I get of being good and sticking to my healthy diet. What is life worth if you can't let go a little once in a while?"

Allie laughed. "All right, I'll take the blame as long as you enjoy yourself."

Anna finished the tea cake in two bites. "Now, have you made any progress in your detective work?"

"No, the police have the file. Sergeant Garret promised to give it back as soon as they're through with it."

"I've just thought of something. Otis had one brother, James, and a sister. I think her name was Olene."

"Was that all of his family? Where did Maude come in?"

"I think she was descended from a sister of Otis' mother or something like that. Not close at all. But Olene had a son, a nice little boy who spent his summers here. I believe he married someone and moved out of state."

Allie selected a chocolate chip cookie. "Did James have children?"

"A boy and a girl, neither one anything to shout about. They were each a chip off the old block. Just like James."

Allie sat wrapped in thought, trying to sort out all of these people. "Renata Aiken claims to be Otis' niece."

Anna bit into a cookie and washed it down with tea. "Great-niece, surely. From James' side of the family. I've never met her, but Eliza thought she was a spoiled, silly woman."

Allie grinned. That jibed with her impression of the haughty Mrs. Aiken. "What did she think of George?"

"She said he was all wind and no weight. Never trusted him any farther than she could throw a Jersey bull."

A car horn sounded out in front, followed shortly by the doorbell. Anna got to her feet. "That's Kady, right on time." She patted Allie's arm. "Don't worry, dear. It will come out just fine in the end. Somehow it always does."

Allie opened the door for Anna and followed her out to the porch. Harry was tying up rose canes by the front fence. Anna stopped, looking puzzled. "Who is that man?"

Allie looked where she indicated. "That's Harry Dalton. He's working for me, doing maintenance. Why? Do you know him?"

Anna shook her head. "I must be losing my mind. For a minute I thought he looked familiar, but I don't know anyone named Dalton."

Allie watched as Kady drove away. No matter how this all turned out, she had met some wonderful friends. Harry had left the roses, and as she settled in the porch swing, he came around the corner of the house carrying pruning shears.

"I'm going to prune the bushes around the carriage house and the guesthouse if that's all right with you."

Allie rocked contentedly in the swing. "Anything you do is all right with me. You've created a wonderland here. This is the prettiest yard in Stony Point, and it's all because of you."

Harry looked uncomfortable. "It's coming along. I saw you had company."

"Anna Milcrest, an old friend of Eliza's. She wanted to see what we had done to the house."

"Saw the Aikens too. What did they want?"

Allie sighed. "They're trying to take the house away from me. Renata was related to Eliza's husband, and she thinks she's entitled to it."

Harry's eyes sparkled with anger. He clashed the blades of the pruning shears together. "Don't you worry, Miss Allie. That four-flusher won't get his hands on this place. I'll see to that, or my name isn't Harry Dalton."

Allie watched him stride away, suddenly more concerned about Harry Dalton than she was about George Aiken. He'd looked downright rabid when he talked about George. She was coming around to Clay's way of thinking. There was more to Harry than met the eye.

Clay had searched the county recorder's office, the library, and everywhere else he could think of for a blueprint of the Ramsdale house. Now he was at the museum, hoping for the best.

Sara Elliston, the blue-haired woman behind the counter, frowned thoughtfully. "You know, I do think we have some blueprints on file somewhere. Now, if I can just think of where they might be."

Clay waited patiently as she dug through file cabinets and searched notebooks while also taking time to answer questions

from other people and give directions to certain displays. He
had about given up when she returned, flushed and disheveled.

"Found them. Someone had packed them away in a box for
some reason."

He hurried to take the cardboard carton from her. "Here, let
me. That's too heavy for you."

She laughed. "You wouldn't think it, but we do a lot of heavy
lifting here. There's always something that needs to be moved
or cleaned, and then we have exhibits coming in."

Sara cleared a space on a sturdy table. "Put them here, and
when you're through looking, we'll put it back in the storage
room."

She left to talk to an elderly man using a cane who had just
entered and stood looking around as if lost. Clay opened the
box and lifted out folder after folder, reading the names. What
a treasure trove. Here were the blueprints for many of the
beautiful old homes in Stony Point.

He'd almost reached the bottom of the box when he found
the folder labeled *Ramsdale*. He carefully stacked the others
back in the box and moved it out of the way. The blueprint was
a work of art to someone like him. He pored over every line,
every note, but in the end he closed the folder, feeling only dis-
appointment. Every door listed was present and accounted for.

Sara came over to join him. "Find what you were looking
for?"

He shook his head. "I found the blueprint, all right, but I
didn't find what I needed to know."

"And that is?"

Clay tapped the folder with one forefinger. "I need to know
if there is a secret door into the Ramsdale house. Someone is
coming and going, and we can't figure out how."

"You mean someone without a key?"

"That's what we think. Only problem is, we can't prove it."

" 'We'? You mean you and Eliza's great-niece?"

"Allie McGregor, yes." Clay rubbed the back of his neck,
feeling weary. "I guess you know Maude Wheeler was killed
in the parlor there."

Sara's voice took on a tinge of acid. "It's a wonder some-one hadn't whacked Maude in the head sooner. I've seldom met a more irritating woman."

Clay laughed. "I guess a lot of people felt that way, but as far as I can tell, none of them had access to the house."

"You know, there is one thing," Sara said. "It's far-fetched, though. Maybe I'm just reaching."

"I've reached a few times myself on this. What is it?"

Sara looked as if she wished she hadn't mentioned it. "You'll think I'm silly."

"I promise I won't. Come on, Sara. I've going crazy trying to find something on this thing. The police think Allie killed Maude."

"Oh, no. That lovely girl." She fidgeted with the band on her wristwatch. "Well, it's just that Missouri was a border state in the Civil War. Some of the people here had very strong feelings for and against slavery."

Clay frowned, not sure where she was going with this.

"I remember reading somewhere that a couple of houses in town were involved in the Underground Railroad."

A glimmer of light penetrated Clay's thoughts. "You mean, maybe . . ."

"Maybe there's not a secret door. Maybe it's a secret tun-nel."

"In that case, it would be well hidden." Clay let that churn around in his mind. "The entrance would be in the basement somewhere but hidden behind something."

"That's what I was thinking," Sara said. "Mind you, there's not a bit of proof."

"It's something to think about, though." Clay tapped the blueprint. "Can I get a copy of this?"

"Surely." Sara picked up the folder. "You know, you might be able to get a book from the library about the Underground Railroad. Maybe it would have some information about this part of the country."

"Good idea." Clay waited until Sara brought him the copy. "I owe you one, Sara."

"You don't owe me anything. Just clear Eliza's niece's name, and I'll be happy."

Clay went from the museum to the library, where he found three books on the Underground Railroad. He carried them out to the car, feeling a minor surge of excitement. At least he felt like he was accomplishing something, although he'd be hard pressed to say exactly what.

Allie worked in the attic, sorting through trunks for vintage clothing Lita could use in her shop. Some of the stuff stored here had to be older than Eliza. Maybe it had come with the house. She lifted out a wedding gown, yellow with age, and marveled at the narrow waist. Ivory satin pumps followed and a delicate veil of Irish lace that went with the gown. She laid these aside, knowing Lita would pay a good price for quality items like this.

"Allie, are you up there? You have a visitor."

A visitor? Who would be calling on her? Surely not George or Renata, or Cora would have been more uptight. Although, come to think of it, there was an odd note in her voice.

Allie got to her feet and started downstairs. Cora waited at the top of the second-floor steps. "Who is it?"

Cora made a face. "It's Howard."

"Howard!" What was he doing here? She looked at her grimy hands. "Let me wash up, and I'll be right down."

Cora nodded and left, and Allie went along to the new bathroom on the second floor. She took her time tidying up. No one had invited Howard to come, and maybe if he cooled his heels long enough, he would take the hint.

Unfortunately, when she went downstairs, he was still there, sitting in the parlor wearing a petulant expression. She noticed that Cora, who was the soul of hospitality, hadn't offered him anything to drink. Showed what she thought of him, all right.

He got to his feet when she entered the room. "Ah, there you are. I was about to give up on you."

"Sorry, I was cleaning in the attic and needed to wash off

the grime." She sat down on the edge of one of the chairs, as far from him as she could get. "This is a surprise."

"I fail to see why. You are my fiancée, after all."

"Oh, no. You don't pull that. I gave your ring back, remember?"

He shrugged. "I never took that seriously. We belong together, and you know it. After all, we dated for four years."

"Right. Four years of you taking and me giving. Look, Howard. I don't know why you're here, but I'm not interested in being your personal assistant anymore."

"Don't be dramatic, please. I may have asked you to do a few things for me, but I can't see why you would object. People in love do things for each other."

"Name one thing you've done for me."

He looked irritated. "Now, come on, Allie. Is that any way to treat me after I drove all the way from St. Louis to see you? Your parents were concerned. They haven't heard from you lately."

"I haven't heard from them either. I assumed they were too busy to stay in touch."

"I think they're waiting for you to come to your senses and return home."

Allie shook her head. "Not this time. I'm staying in Stony Point and operating a bed-and-breakfast." She had a good idea why her parents hadn't called. Howard, the kind, affectionate man who wanted so badly to be their son-in-law, had persuaded them that Allie just needed a little time to come to her senses. She felt anger burning in the pit of her stomach.

He looked around at the antique furniture, the fresh paint. "I had no idea the house would be anything like this. Forget all that nonsense about a bed-and-breakfast. It would be a perfect place to live."

She knew he was visualizing himself as master of the house. Well, she could let the wind out of that little balloon right now. "I assume you've heard that a woman was murdered in this room just a few days ago. As far as the police are concerned, I'm the prime suspect."

His face paled. "You can't be serious."

"I'm very serious. Maybe it's good you came after all. I need all the support I can get."

He looked at her as if she were delirious. "I see. Unfortunately, I must return to St. Louis this afternoon." He got to his feet. "It has been nice seeing you again. I'll tell your parents you are looking well."

"You do that." She followed him in his rush for the door, realizing she had just seen the last of Howard. He wasn't the sort to get involved in anything even slightly resembling a murder investigation. Not like Clay, who was willing to move mountains to clear her name.

Cora peeked out of the office. "Has he gone?"

"Yep. Running like a rabbit, afraid he might get caught up in a murder investigation."

Cora looked belligerent. "Don't you spend any time worrying about him. He's not good enough for you."

Allie laughed. "You know, I think you're right. I forgot to ask, did Roger list us with a reservation service agency?"

Cora smiled, eyes twinkling. "He sure did, and he wants to go over our accounts and make sure we're in good shape for tax time. It seems he was a CPA before he moved back here. In fact, he's thinking of opening his own office."

"And he can be our accountant!" Allie exclaimed. "Oh, Cora, if we could get this mess straightened out, we could open up and start getting customers."

"Give it time," Cora cautioned. "We're getting there, and the police will solve this case. I know they will."

Allie poured herself a glass of tea. "Well, I just hope they don't think I'm part of the solution."

Clay stared at the page, almost too tired to think. He'd been reading for three hours now, just taking time off to go to the bathroom. There it was. He'd finally found it. The Ramsdale house—or the Gordon house, as it was known then—*had* been part of the Underground Railroad. Now he just had to find the entrance.

He leaned back and closed his eyes. He'd tried everything else, so he might as well look for that tunnel. He realized that finding it might take a miracle, but he had to try for Allie's sake. He didn't know how she had become such an important part of his life, but there was no denying his feelings for her. He had no idea how she felt about him, and it didn't matter. The main thing was to get her off the hook in this murder case and keep her safe from whoever was trying to destroy her.

He inserted a bookmark between the pages and closed the book. Tomorrow he'd show Joe Garret what he'd found.

Chapter Thirteen

Allie finished balancing her checkbook and stared in dismay at the total. If they didn't open for business before long and have some money coming in, she would have to start looking for a job. The work on restoring the house had taken a big bite out of the money Aunt Eliza had left, although Clay had cut corners every way he could, and she suspected he'd done a lot of work without putting it on the tab. Whenever she asked about it, though, he denied it, saying he'd gotten the supplies wholesale.

She leaned back in her chair, letting her eyes survey the office. Cora had done wonders with it, making the room businesslike but attractive. Allie smiled, thinking one of the smartest things she had ever done was befriend Cora Witner. She hadn't known how badly she needed someone to rely on. How badly they needed each other, she amended.

Blakely had been quiet, not calling or bothering his sister, but Cora had heard from John Bailey that Cora's half brother was considering settling out of court, dividing the property between them. Evidently he was afraid of being made to look like a miser by cutting Cora out of everything. People who knew the family knew how hard she had worked taking care of her parents, and they were angry on her behalf, faulting Blakely.

Allie put the books away and stopped by the kitchen for a glass of water. Taz lay stretched out on the floor, guarding his feed dish. Poor Taz. He'd never gotten over sharing the kitchen with Dinah. Although the cat stayed at the guesthouse now, the pup wasn't taking any chances.

She drained the glass and set it on the countertop. "Hey, pal. I'm going up to my room. Want to come?"

He watched impassively until she turned to leave, then got to his feet and trotted after her. She scooped him into her arms and carried him up the steps. He navigated the stairs more easily now, but they were still a chore for him.

In her room, Allie picked up the photo album she had found in the attic. She'd intended to inspect it more thoroughly but hadn't had the chance. Now she carried it to the small table by the window and spread it out, slowly turning the pages, looking for anyone she recognized.

There they were, those gone but not forgotten ancestors she had never known existed. Eliza, young, smiling at the camera in casual shots, beautiful and slightly regal in the more formal, posed photographs. Allie stared at the laughing eyes, the smiling lips, and wished she'd known her back then. Which was foolish; she hadn't even been born yet.

There was James, and he did look like Otis. If you didn't know either one very well, you probably could get them confused. Score one for Eliza. She got that right. From all Allie had heard about James, he'd probably be capable of stealing, but would he let his own brother take the blame?

Olene, Otis' sister, was pretty in a washed-out kind of way, the sort who would probably have trouble speaking up for herself. Allie decided she was making a lot of judgments based on an old photo. Other pictures showed Olene looking more confident. A picture of a young boy caught her attention. A cute little guy, he grinned at the camera, looking full of mischief the way little boys do. Allie turned the page, then turned back, curious. Something about him reminded her of someone. She eased the picture out of the black paper corners holding it in the album and turned it over. There, in spidery handwriting, was the reason she thought she knew him.

Harry Dalton, age seven. Olene's son.

Allie stared in disbelief at the words. Harry Dalton was related to Otis? Was he another who thought the house should belong to him? She looked out the window at the beds of abundant flowers, the herb garden tended so lovingly, and thought how much she liked Harry.

Why had he lied to her? She stopped and thought about that. No. Harry hadn't lied; he just hadn't told the entire truth. He never said he wasn't related to Otis; he'd just never admitted he was. Anna had thought he looked familiar, but she didn't recognize the name. But at her age names must be hard to remember sometimes.

Allie inserted the picture back into the album and turned the page, not recognizing anyone there. A few pages later she found more pictures of Eliza and Otis. She tried to imagine them living in this house, laughing and loving, flesh and blood instead of faded pictures in a long-ago album, but the images wouldn't come.

On the last page she found a family group picture. She removed it from the album and turned it over to see if the names had been written on the back. The people seemed to be members of James' family, and she tried to match the names to the person, plowing through all the Ramsdales until she hit a name that stopped her.

Noah Olson? She turned the picture over and looked curiously at the man who matched that name. Medium height, medium looks, nothing special compared to the more handsome Ramsdales. She turned to the back again, searching for a name, certain she would find it.

Lottie Olson. Mary Olson.

Allie stared blindly at the open window. Mary was a relative too. She remembered how the mousy little woman had kept saying that Maude didn't have a right to the house. Apparently she was a closer relative to Otis than Maude had been. Allie sighed. Harry, Renata, Mary, Maude—relatives were coming out of the woodwork. Except they weren't related to her. She was the only one descended from Eliza, and Eliza had owned the house. Therefore Eliza had a right to leave it to her great-niece if she so chose. Otis' descendents would have just to get over it.

Allie closed the album and decided to go to the attic to look for Eliza's picture that Anna had mentioned. She was determined to find the portrait and hang it back over the parlor fireplace where it belonged.

The attic was hot and airless, but she searched, although not putting all that much effort into it. Taz, who had followed her up the stairs, lay slumped near the door, sleeping. As she watched, he raised his head, ears perked. He got to his feet, stalking stiff-legged toward the door.

Allie followed him, trying to walk quietly. Was someone in the house? It wouldn't be Cora. She and Roger had gone out. Clay had a key, and so did Cora, but as far as she knew, no one else did. She crept down the stairs until she reached the first floor. The house seemed empty, felt empty. Maybe it was just a false alarm.

Taz stopped at the door leading down to the basement. Allie hesitated. She didn't want to go down there alone. What if she fell on the rickety steps? Would anyone find her? Taz growled softly, as if he wasn't sure he wanted to be heard.

Allie took a deep breath. This would never do. If someone was prowling in the cellar, she needed to check it out. She picked up Cora's rolling pin from the crock holding kitchen utensils and carefully opened the door. Taz hung back as she descended the stairs. The basement was clean, thanks to Cora, and dry. Light filtered in through the narrow windows located at the top of the walls.

At the foot of the steps Allie halted, looking around. As far as she could see, nothing was out of place. She waited, muscles tensed, senses tuned. The basement didn't feel empty the way the upper floors had. A slight sound, like rustling cloth, sounded from behind her. She started to turn, but something crashed against her skull. Pain, accompanied by a blinding flash of light. Allie dropped like a felled tree.

Clay drove to the police station, hoping he could convince Joe Garret that the research he'd done was reliable. Joe was a levelheaded, practical man. It might be hard to persuade him to look for a tunnel Clay had no proof even existed.

He found the policeman at his desk. "Hi, Clay. I was just going to give you a call."

"Yeah? What's up?"

"Did you know that Maude Wheeler was related to Otis Ramsdale?"

Clay sat down and placed his manila folder of papers on the desk. "You sure about that? It might explain why she was so positive she had a right to the house."

Joe nodded. "Her and Renata Aiken. Wonder how many more there are. I guess I need to do some research."

"Got it right here." Clay tapped the file. "Already done your work for you. Don't bother to thank me."

"All right, I won't," Joe said. "What do you have there?"

"For starters, I didn't find out much about the family, but I did learn that the Ramsdale house was part of the Underground Railroad during the Civil War."

Joe looked puzzled. "Is that supposed to mean something to me?"

"If I remember right, you slept through history in school. It means there might be a tunnel leading from the house to somewhere outside."

"A tunnel? You mean you think someone is entering the house through a secret tunnel? Do you really expect me to believe that?"

"I expect you to at least consider it." Clay took the pages he had copied from the file and handed them over. "Look, there has to be another entrance."

"No, there doesn't have to be. Allie McGregor could have done every one of those things she claimed happened. You weren't watching her every minute. Neither was Cora. How much trouble would it be to move a few items around, write some words on a mirror, claim to have had a phone call?"

"You didn't see her when we discovered those things. She was scared."

"Maybe she's a good actress." Joe leaned back in his chair. "Look, I'm sorry. I know you've got it bad for her. . . ."

"Who said I did?"

Joe shook his head in exasperation. "No one had to tell me. Man! We get to the house, and there you are. We look around the crime scene, and you're looking over our shoulder. We go out to check the house for exits, and there you are again. You're like an old mama duck with one duckling. It sticks out all over you."

Clay figured he might as well not answer that. This was one of those situations where the less said, the less could come back to haunt him. "Never mind about that. Just look at what I've got here. Now, according to this book, the Ramsdale house was part of the Underground Railroad helping slaves escape to the North, where they'd be safe."

"All right, we'll consider that's correct for the sake of the argument. So where does that leave us?"

"I'm not sure, but I think it's entirely possible that there's an outside tunnel where they could smuggle people inside and hide them in the cellar."

Joe looked at Clay's notes. "You know, it's hard to believe something like this ever happened. That men and women made in the likeness of God were bought and sold. I admire the ones who risked their lives to bring that filthy practice to an end."

Clay nodded. "Slavery was a dark blot on the history of America, no doubt about it. I think the Gordons, who lived there at that time, tried to do something to help, and that's why I believe there is an old tunnel that someone knows about and is using to get in and out of the house without being detected."

Joe leaned forward, arms on the desk, and Clay thought he was getting interested in spite of himself. "Okay, say you're right. We were in that basement. Where would they hide the tunnel entrance?"

"It would have to be someplace with easy access," Clay said. "If the people they were hiding needed to leave in a hurry, they'd want to get out of there with as little hassle as possible."

"Maybe we'd better take another look at that basement," Joe said.

Clay's cell phone rang. He answered to find Harry, sounding agitated. "Slow down. I can't tell what you're saying."

After a minute he said, "I'll be right there."

He clicked the phone off and rose, kicking his chair back out of the way. "Let's go. Allie's disappeared."

Joe was on his feet. "We'll take the squad car—it'll be quicker."

Clay got into the passenger seat as Joe slammed the door on the driver's side. They zoomed from the parking lot, siren blaring. Cars scattered as tourists navigating the narrow streets tried to get out of the way. Clay braced himself as they zipped around a corner. He'd always wanted a ride like this, wondering how it would feel to have the siren screaming in your ears. Now he was too worried to enjoy it.

"Harry say anything helpful?" Joe asked.

"Not much. Just that her car was there, her purse was upstairs in her room, and she was gone. Her dog is throwing a fit, though."

"Hmm." Joe squeaked the cruiser between a pickup truck and a Volkswagen. "Well, we'll see what we find when we get there."

Clay reflected that if Joe kept driving the way he was, it would be a miracle if they ended up anywhere except in the hospital. The siren died to a thin wail as they drove between the wrought-iron gates and stopped in front of the Ramsdale house.

Harry met them on the porch. "I've looked everywhere I can think of, and not a sign of her. But that dog is going berserk. I think he knows something."

"Pity he can't tell us." Cora joined them, holding a struggling Taz in her arms. "I've fought him till I'm exhausted."

They stepped into the foyer, and Joe motioned to the pup. "Put him down, and let's see what he does."

Cora set the puppy down on the polished parquet floor, and he ran toward the pantry so fast, his toenails scrabbled across the wooden surface. They followed, stopping as Taz scratched at the door leading to the basement and erupted into a frenzy of barking. Clay opened the door, and the dog plunged through, lost his balance on the first step, and rolled down the short flight of wooden stairs.

Cora picked up the puppy, cuddling him and talking in soothing tones, but he squirmed in her arms, and she put him down on the concrete floor. Taz ran across the room to a set of shelves holding fruit jars, sniffing and whining. Clay leaned against the shelves, trying to swing them out from the wall, but they wouldn't budge. He looked up to see Harry approaching with an axe in his hands.

Chapter Fourteen

Allie's eyelashes fluttered open, then closed again. Gradually she became more aware of her surroundings. She lay flat on her back on something cold and hard . . . and damp, staring at a slab of concrete with a spiderweb of cracks stretching overhead like a roof. After a moment she pushed herself up onto one elbow, waiting until the room stopped whirling. A large black bug ran over her hand. She bit back a scream, startled by the scratchy movement against her skin. She turned her head slowly, eyeing the concrete walls where the plaster had fallen away in places to reveal the wet earth behind the patchy interior.

A thicket of brush blocked a narrow opening—the fresh green of new leaves allowed a flickering light to penetrate the dim interior. She sniffed. The air smelled musty, tinged with mold. A cellar? Her probing gaze took in the packed earthen floor, the closed wooden door studding one wall.

Allie forced herself to remember. She had gone down to the basement. Heard a noise. Something hit her on the head, and she woke up here . . . wherever here was. Another thought occurred to her. The person who had left her might very well come back. Groaning from the effort, she forced herself to her knees, then managed to pull herself up to her feet.

A shadow darkened the entrance. A pale hand parted the bushes, and a slight form pushed through, dark against the glimmering light of the opening. Allie's heartbeat accelerated. She shrank back against the wall, terribly aware that the ancient cellar provided no hiding place.

166

"Ah. You're awake." Mary Olson spoke in a matter-of-fact tone, as if it were the most natural thing in the world to be meeting in a cold, dank cellar. "I was afraid I hit you too hard."

"What do you want with me?" Allie was surprised to hear the words come out as little more than a croak. She cleared her throat and tried again. "Why am I in this place?"

"Because I put you here, of course," Mary said. "That should be perfectly obvious."

"But why? I never did anything to you."

"Of course you did," Mary scolded. "Don't try to pretend you don't know what I'm talking about either. Sneaking in and buttering up Eliza so she'd leave you the house that should have come to me."

Allie sighed in frustration. She should have taken her father's advice and had nothing to do with Otis' family. And speaking of the Ramsdale clan, there were entirely too many of them to suit her.

"Why do you think you deserved the house any more than Maude or Renata . . . or Harry?"

Mary blinked. "Harry? Who's Harry?"

Allie swallowed, her throat dry and scratchy. "Harry Dalton, Olene Ramsdale's son."

"He has nothing to do with this. I haven't seen him in years. Wouldn't know him if I met him on the street."

"You knew Maude and Renata. They're your cousins."

Mary shook her head. "Maude was a distant relative, hardly no kin at all."

"What about Renata?" Allie asked. "She's related to you. Where does she come in?"

"My uncle Edwin's granddaughter. A silly woman. Grandpa James wouldn't have cared for her." The words tumbled out of Mary, her voice rising. A nervous tic jerked the corner of her eyelid.

"Not like you?" Allie asked, trying to calm her. "I'll bet you're never silly."

Mary's agitated expression eased. "Not at all like me," she

bragged. "I know what I want and how to go after it. Grandpa James taught me that."

So Mary's mother must have been James' daughter. That would make Renata her second cousin, which would explain the wide gap in their ages. Nothing, however, explained Mary's behavior. She swung irrationally from anger to almost abstraction.

"What about Maude?" *Keep her talking.* Surely someone would come looking for them. This cellar couldn't be too far from the house. Mary wouldn't have been physically capable of carrying her for a long distance. Although, judging from the way she felt, *dragging* might be more accurate.

Mary's features twisted in an angry grimace. "I told her to stop calling it her house, but she wouldn't listen. She wasn't even a Ramsdale. Not like me. I was Otis' own niece."

"So you killed her?"

"She kept talking about the changes she would make. She knew I was upset, but Maude wouldn't care how anyone else felt." Mary clenched and unclenched her hands. Her lips thinned to a narrow line.

"You hit her with the poker." Allie could feel the strength returning to limbs that had been numb. If she could keep Mary talking for a while longer, maybe she could manage to overwhelm her captor and escape. Once out of the cellar, surely she could reach safety.

"I just meant to scare her," Mary said. Her anger faded, making her look more mouselike than ever. "I never meant to hurt Maude, not really. I just swung the poker, and she slumped over with blood running down her face." She sounded lost, almost unsure of herself.

"Where are we, Mary?" Allie spoke softly. "How did you get me here?"

"We're in an old abandoned cellar." She answered readily enough, although she seemed to be listening for something.

Allie suppressed a shudder. "Whose cellar?" It had to be somewhere close to the house.

Mary indicated the old wooden slab on one wall. "That

door opens into a tunnel that joins this cellar with the basement in Eliza's house."

"Did Maude know about the tunnel?"

"Not until the night I brought her here. She didn't believe I could get into the house. I had to show her."

"Renata doesn't know about it?"

"You think Renata would crawl through a dirty tunnel and play pranks on you? She has a rich husband to buy houses for her. She doesn't have to do the things I've done just to claim what's rightfully mine." Mary's voice held a world of bitterness.

"So you're the one who moved things around?"

"And wrote the messages."

"And the phone calls?" Allie asked.

"No, that was Maude. She got someone to make those calls for her."

Allie leaned against the clammy concrete wall, still having trouble believing their secret visitor was this small, ungainly woman. And yet, she had killed Maude in a fit of irritation, even if she claimed it was an accident. What about motive? What was behind her strange behavior?

Allie put her question into words. "Why, Mary? What did you hope to gain by doing those things?"

"Why, scare you into leaving, of course. Once you were gone, I could live in the house where I belonged."

Mary's matter-of-fact reply chilled Allie, although she tried not to show her creeping anxiety. "I don't see how you expected that to work. I couldn't afford to walk away now that I've put all of this money into restoring the house. Too much to write off, and I assume you can't afford to buy me out."

"I can as soon as I find my grandpa's jewels." Mary's eyes shone with a fanatical light. "They're in the basement of the Ramsdale house, where Grandpa James hid them."

Allie had forgotten about the jewels. Truth be told, she had taken the stories of stolen treasure as a sort of local urban legend. Yet here was Mary, talking as if they actually existed. "He hid them in Otis' house? Why would he do that?"

"Actually, it was a good place—or it would have been if Eliza had treated us the way we deserved."

"Your grandfather let Otis go to jail for something he didn't do? That's terrible. So Eliza was right after all."

Mary's face flushed with anger. "That woman refused to allow Grandpa James to set foot in his own brother's house. Then he was killed in a car wreck and never had a chance to recover what was his."

Allie tried to bring a note of reason to the conversation. "But, Mary, even if you find the jewels, they don't belong to you. They belong to the former owners or the insurance company."

"Of course they're mine. They belonged to my grandfather, and I'm his oldest surviving grandchild."

"But he stole them!"

Mary drew herself up, looking affronted. "My grandpa was not a thief. If you leave valuable things lying around and don't take care of what you own, you can't blame someone for taking them. Besides, taking things is just borrowing without asking permission."

Allie sighed. This logic was beyond her. A frantic scratching against the wooden door brought her whirling around. A whimper, an excited bark. *Taz.*

Mary clapped her hands together in frustration. "I should have killed that dog when I had the chance, instead of putting him upstairs. How did he get into the tunnel anyway? I'm sure I closed the opening behind me."

Kill Taz? Allie's heart contracted. Not if she could help it. Someone had to have let the pup into the tunnel. She turned her head to listen, trying to hear over Taz's barking while edging toward the opening. If she could just get outside, she could scream for help.

Mary laughed. "Don't even think about it. Before you forced your way through that brush blocking the entrance, I'd catch you. We're leaving, but you'll do it my way."

Clay stared open-mouthed as Harry walked toward him, swinging the axe gently from side to side. *What now?* He'd known all along that there was something strange about the man. Had Harry lured them down here for a massacre?

Harry took a stance and drew back the axe. "Step aside, Clay, and hold that dog. I'll bust these shelves apart."

"Wait!" Cora yelled. "Get those jars out of the way. You hit them with that axe, and they'll shatter. The flying glass will cut you to ribbons."

Harry glared at her. "Get on with it, then. We've got to hurry if we want to save that girl."

"That sounds like you know something about this," Joe said. "You got anything to tell us?"

"I don't have time to stand around and chat. That's the trouble with you boys in uniform—all talk and no action. And if there ever was a time to move, this is it. You want to help save that girl, or you want to stand around jawing until she's dead?"

"You know who's got her, don't you?" Joe asked.

"I've got an idea, and if I'm right, we got a problem. That woman is crazier than a fruit fly. We've got to get to them while we still have time."

Joe stared hard at him before nodding. "All right. We'll play it your way for now."

Cora and Clay had been busy removing jars. Now that the shelves were empty, Clay could see a small knob located at the back of the top shelf. He closed his fingers around it and pulled, praying this was the latch. A cracking sound, like an un-oiled hinge, brought Harry and Joe to stand beside him.

Clay pulled harder. "Come on! Open."

The shelf swung back so fast, he almost toppled over. Taz leaped from Cora's arms and raced through the opening.

Joe Garret dashed for the stairs, calling over his shoulder. "We need a light. I'll get mine."

Clay peered into the dark hole, breathing in the scent of damp and mold and something else—a faint fragrance of flowers. Allie's perfume. She had been here.

Joe clambered down the stairs carrying the light. He pushed past Clay. "You stay here. This is my job."

"Forget it. I'm coming. Don't get in my way." Clay bent over and squeezed through the narrow tunnel. From the scuffling noise behind him he knew Harry was hot on his heels, probably carrying his axe. It sounded like Cora was right behind him.

Joe grunted and fell back. "Man! Watch out for that rock." He rubbed his head, indicating a sharp-edged slab of limestone jutting out from the wall. Once they had all seen it, he trained the light on the ground and hurried on down the tunnel.

Clay's heart raced so hard, he fancied he could hear it beating in tandem with his footsteps. Up ahead Taz began to whine, then burst into a flurry of barks. Clay held his breath, listening, but he couldn't hear anything over Taz's yapping. Harry's fear was proving contagious. Clay couldn't bear it if anything happened to Allie. He'd never intended to fall in love—it had caught him when he wasn't looking. Now he couldn't imagine life without her. Why hadn't he ever told her how much she meant to him?

The tunnel ended at a sturdy wooden door where Taz, who had given up barking, was now sitting on his haunches, nose pointed skyward and howling on a mournful note that sent a shiver up Clay's spine.

"Taz! Stop that."

The pup turned his head to look in Clay's direction, then pointed his nose skyward. *Ahooo!*

Cora picked him up, and he struggled to get down, but at least he had stopped howling. Joe backed off and took a few running steps to slam his shoulder against the door. He hit it with a solid *thunk,* which must have jarred the breath out of his body but didn't budge the door one bit. Clay jiggled the doorknob. Locked. From the ray of the flashlight he could see tears on Cora's cheeks and knew she shared his fear.

Harry shoved him aside. "Let me at it. I'll bust it apart." He drew back the axe and hit the door with a solid *thwack.* A few more blows and the wood splintered. Harry swung the axe one more time, and the lock gave way. Clay burst through the door, followed by the others. A cellar, small, damp, and . . . empty.

Taz struggled, catching Cora unaware. She dropped him, and he scrambled to his feet, scurrying toward the opening.

"After him!" Harry yelled. "He knows where Allie is."

The brush at the entrance impeded their progress, but once they burst through, they were in a wooded area, which Clay recognized as the ravine bordering the Ramsdale house. Taz had disappeared in the underbrush, and Clay stopped, listening, not sure where to go. In the distance they heard one sharp puppy bark, then silence.

"That way!" Harry shouted, stumbling off down the hillside. Clay plunged past him, heart pounding. One refrain kept running through his head. *I have to get there in time to save her!*

Allie stumbled after Mary, half falling over rocks and brush, her arm caught in a bruising, viselike grip. Mary apparently had no trouble with the rocky terrain, but then, she knew where she was going, and she didn't have someone dragging her along.

Allie stopped, pulling back against the iron grip. "Wait. I have to get my breath." A stitch had developed in her side, and her head throbbed like a bongo drum.

"We don't have time to stop. Thanks to that dog, they'll be after us."

"Where are you taking me?"

"Someplace only I know about. It would have been better if I could have left you in the cellar, but perhaps this is best after all. You won't be so easily discovered."

Allie jerked backward, trying to break loose. "Stop it, Mary. This is unnecessary. I'm no threat to you."

"This is your own fault, you know," Mary said, the very reasonableness of her voice making the words even more frightening. "I tried to get you to leave, but you wouldn't. You're so stubborn, just like her."

"Like who?" Allie was too winded to think straight. This conversation seemed to be going around in circles, leaving her dizzy.

"Eliza. She wouldn't leave either. Stayed cooped up in the house and wouldn't let me in. Me, Otis' own niece."

"That was just her way," Allie said, feeling a need to defend her great-aunt. "She wouldn't let me into the house either."

"She shouldn't have treated me like that," Mary said. "I could have stayed with her, taken care of her, but she laughed in my face when I suggested it."

Her voice drifted off into a mumbling monologue. "Said she didn't want anything to do with me. I showed her, though. Don't mess with me. That's what Grandpa James always said."

"Showed who?" Allie asked. "Who are you talking about?"

"Eliza, of course." Mary sounded surprised. "Pay attention."

"What did you show Eliza?" The conversation was again going around in circles.

"Why, I found the tunnel and got into the house in spite of her. Do you know it only takes a few minutes to die if someone puts a pillow over your face?"

Allie stared at her, not sure if she had heard right. "You . . . You killed Eliza?"

"It was her own fault, just like it was with Maude. She should have been nicer to me. I was her niece. Same as you."

Allie bit her lip, fighting a rising tide of panic.

Although Mary claimed she hadn't intended to kill Maude, she had just admitted to deliberately taking Eliza's life. This woman was a killing machine.

"Don't you want to know what's going to happen to you?" Mary asked.

Nothing was going to happen if she could help it. She was becoming stronger with every minute. The dizziness had faded, and, given the opportunity, she was going to take this woman down.

Mary's expression changed, becoming morose. A hint of self-pity tinged her voice. "I liked Maude. I never wanted to hurt her, but she just pushed me aside as if I didn't matter. You know what she was like."

"Yes, I know." Allie leaned against a sapling dogwood tree, taking deep breaths. *Just a few minutes more.*

Mary's expression changed, becoming more belligerent.

"She shouldn't have treated me that way. What happened was her own fault."

Allie stepped away from the tree, trying to speak with authority. "Mary, give yourself up. You can't run forever."

"What are you thinking?" Mary cried. "Give myself up just when I'm about to get what I want? I suppose you think I don't matter either. You're just like Maude." She motioned down the trail. "Let's go—get moving."

"I need to rest," Allie said. "I can't run as fast as you do."

"You're playing for time, but it won't do you any good. If you try to get away from me, I'll catch you, and then you'll be sorry you gave me any trouble. I'm stronger than you are because I've consulted the spirits, and I know I'm right on this."

Allie refused to move, although she knew this was just a minor rebellion on her part. Mary was right about one thing: she probably was the stronger of the two. Being knocked on the head and dragged through the woods had taken a toll, although she was starting to recover. If she could only stall Mary long enough, she might be able to escape.

"They'll come looking for me. You won't get away with this. If you're smart, you'll quit while you can."

Mary gripped Allie's shoulder so hard, she almost cried out. "You hush that kind of talk."

The smaller woman's strength was surprising. That and her casual dismissal of Eliza's murder made her appear to be a more formidable opponent than she had seemed at first. She shoved Allie ahead of her. "I don't want to hear any more out of you. Don't look back, and don't stop until I tell you to."

They stumbled down a brush-covered hillside, and Allie could hear the murmur of traffic off to the right, separated from them by a steep, wooded hillside. The path ended at what used to be a home site. Only the low, crumbled walls of a foundation remained. Mary pushed her toward a small rock building set against the side of the hill. A stout wooden door barred the entrance.

She lifted the iron latch. "In here."

"No." Allie had just come from one underground prison. She wasn't going to willingly enter another.

Frustration showed on Mary's face. "Don't argue with me. I'm not going to hurt you. It's just until you sign the deed."

"What deed?"

"Why, the deed giving me the house, of course."

"And then what?"

A look of cunning crossed her features. "Then I'll let you go."

Allie realized that wasn't true. She knew too much to be allowed an opportunity to talk. If she entered that place, she would die there.

"Where will you get the deed?" Allie asked. "Who will prepare it for you?"

For the first time Mary looked uncertain. "That's none of your business," she blurted.

A scattering of loose rocks, a scamper of feet, and a small black body hurtled toward them, growling like an animal twice his size. Taz ignored Allie, charging straight at Mary, teeth bared.

"Get out of here, dog." Mary drew back her foot and kicked out, sending Taz flying. The pup yelped in pain. Anger rocketed through Allie. That was her dog, and no one was going to mistreat him.

Mary grabbed a stick and strode toward the injured puppy. "Leave me alone, you worthless cur."

Allie caught her by the arm and jerked her backward. "Don't you dare hit my dog."

Mary, taken by surprise, dropped the stick. She curved her fingers into claws as she lunged. Allie met her halfway, one arm lifted to ward off the attack. Their bodies slammed together, and Allie shoved her attacker backward. Mary stumbled over a large stone. Off balance, she went down, dragging Allie with her.

"To the right!" Joe shouted. "There's an old house down that path."

Clay scrambled over the rocky trail. In the distance, Taz

yelped in pain. Angry voices, like people arguing, sent him running faster. *Allie's voice!* He'd know it anywhere. She was alive.

Clay dodged through a sumac thicket and leaped over a fallen log. The others scurried after him. He heard a crash behind him as someone slipped and went down. He hoped it wasn't Cora, but he didn't have time to stop. He plunged around a curve in the path and saw two figures scuffling on the ground.

By the time he reached them, Allie had Mary spread-eagled in the path, sitting on her. Taz had his teeth locked on the older woman's jacket sleeve, paws braced and growling furiously. Clay grinned. That was one disturbed pup. He helped Allie to her feet, drawing her into the shelter of his arms.

"Are you all right?"

She tried to pull away from him. "Don't let her escape."

"She won't. Joe and Harry will see to that."

His arms tightened around her. As soon as he got this woman someplace private, he was going to tell her just how much he loved her and that he was never going to let her go.

He was dimly aware of Joe and Harry handcuffing a spitting, squawking Mary Olson. Her white hair, loosened from the knot at the back of her head, straggled around her face, giving her a wild appearance.

"Leave me alone!" she screeched. "What do you think you're doing?"

"I'm arresting you for kidnapping, resisting arrest, and anything else I can come up with." Joe grunted as a well-aimed kick connected with his shin. "Ow! Cut that out."

"Murder," Allie said.

"What?" Joe asked. "Who, Maude?"

"And Eliza." She leaned against Clay, as if the admission had hurt her.

"Eliza too?" Joe looked stunned.

Harry strode forward. "You killed Eliza, did you? I wish I'd known that earlier."

"Cut that out," Joe said. "Maybe she did, and maybe she didn't, but either way, she'll pay for it. Don't do anything stupid."

They walked back to the house, Clay supporting Allie. Joe had a firm grip on Mary, and Cora carried Taz. Harry brought up the rear, still furious and grumbling under his breath.

"I'm taking Allie to the hospital," Cora said. "She needs to have that head wound checked."

Allie started to protest, but Joe cut her off. "You go on. A blow to the head is serious, and we won't need you here for now. You'd just be in the way."

"I'm going with her," Clay began.

"Oh, no, you're not," Joe interrupted. "I need to talk to you and to Harry. I'm going to get a crime team out to look over the place, and I want you right here."

Was he serious? Just because they'd been friends since high school didn't give him the right to throw his weight around. "You can't keep me here."

"Watch me, buddy." Joe met him glare for glare, while Mary protested his increasingly firm grasp. "I've got a kidnapping and one, possibly two, murders on my hands, and no one is going to mess it up for me. Cora can go with Allie. You stay here."

"And if I don't?"

"Oh, you will. If I have to, I'll put you under arrest for obstructing the investigation of a crime. If necessary, I'll cuff you to a table leg. We straight on this now?"

"Sure. Fine." Clay slumped down in a chair and watched as Allie followed Cora from the room. He didn't say anything until after Joe had called in his backup and they came to take Mary away.

Chapter Fifteen

Clay sat at the kitchen table, still out of sorts. He didn't know why Joe thought it was so necessary to keep him here. After all, he didn't know any more than Harry did.

"Relax," Joe said. "She'll be safe in the ER, and you'll see her soon enough. You might as well be here helping me instead of sitting in a waiting room at the hospital."

"That's right, Clay," Harry said. "We've got work to do right here."

"And we're starting with you, Harry." Joe pointed to a chair. "Sit. We've got some talking to do."

Clay watched as Harry sat down and placed his clasped hands on the table, interested in spite of himself. He'd suspected all along that there was something off about the guy. Joe was right. It was time to get the truth out on the table.

"Okay, see, Otis was my uncle," Harry began. "I was just a kid, and both of my parents worked, so I spent my summers with Otis and Eliza. She was one sweet woman."

"So you're another relative," Clay said, disgusted.

"Hey, I'm not like those from James' other side of the family. They were a bunch of crooks from the get-go."

"Then what are you doing here if you're not trying to take the house away from Allie?"

"I don't want the place. Eliza had a right to do what she wanted with it, especially after what James did to Otis."

"Then what do you want?" Joe asked. "I'm assuming you have a reason for being here."

179

"The same thing the others want," Harry said defensively. "The jewels James Ramsdale stole and hid in this house."

"Jewels?" Joe looked skeptical. "I've always figured that if they did exist, they were long gone."

Clay silently agreed with him.

"Oh, they existed, all right." Harry stared down at his clasped hands. "See, James was a crook, pure and simple, and he brought his kids up to be the same. My mother, now . . ." He looked defiantly at them. "She wasn't that way. Her and Otis were both decent, hardworking people."

Joe scribbled a few notes. "Okay now, you think the jewels are hidden here?"

"I know they're here," Harry said. "So do the others. That's why they're trying to run Allie off, and it's what got Maude killed."

Joe tapped his pen against a small notebook. "How are you so sure about all of this?"

Harry cupped his chin in one hand, fingers covering his mouth, as if thinking. After a moment he sighed and shrugged. "Okay, I guess I probably couldn't have taken them anyway. You can't go against your family, or at least you shouldn't. Olene Dalton was an honest woman, and I'll not be letting her down."

Clay watched him, looking for any sign of deception, but as far as he could tell, Harry was finally coming clean.

"James got mixed up with a woman who fancied herself a writer. She wrote a book about the history of Stony Point, and she included this house, only she didn't call it this house."

"Huh?" Joe looked puzzled. "Come again?"

"She gave it a false name instead of calling it the Ramsdale house, that right?" Clay suggested.

"Bingo!" Harry pointed a finger at him. "But see, I spent a lot of time here when I was a kid, and like kids do, I prowled over every inch of this place, so I recognized it right away."

"Why did you just now show up?" Joe asked skeptically. "Seems to me if you were on such good terms with Eliza, you had ready access to the house."

"Oh, I did," Harry agreed. "I visited her when I could,

which wasn't often, since I had to make a living, but I didn't know about the jewels being here until I read the book."

"And you got the book where?" Clay asked. This was sounding more and more like a work of fiction.

"Bought a box of junk at a garage sale that had some books in it. I knew about James' connection with the woman, so I read the book, and there it was."

"And you think you can show us where the jewels are?" Joe asked.

"Well, the general vicinity. James wasn't fool enough to tell her exactly where they were, but we can look."

"I guess there's no time like the present." Joe got to his feet. "You ready?"

"Sure." Harry stood up and grinned. "I'd sort of hoped to do my hunting a little more private-like, but this will do."

The three of them trooped down to the basement, where Harry stood looking around, as if not sure what to do next. "Well, let's see. I know they're in the basement somewhere. All we have to do is find them."

He took a folded piece of paper out of his pocket. "Seven steps straight ahead. Ten steps to the right." He paced them off and ended against the basement wall.

"Now what?" Clay asked. This seemed like a kid's treasure hunt to him. He still had his doubts that the jewels existed.

"I don't know." Harry scratched his head. "I figured there'd be a loose brick or something."

"Let me see those directions." Clay read them, looking for a clue. Suddenly he saw the problem. "Seven steps in what direction?" he asked.

"What?" Harry grabbed the paper from him. "It doesn't say which direction?"

"So where does that leave us?" Joe asked.

"We'll just start over. I'll face this way." Harry walked the required steps, which left him standing in the middle of the floor.

Four tries later they were no closer to finding the jewels. "One more time," Harry declared. He paced off in a new direction, and his shoulders sagged. "I was so sure I could find them."

Clay rolled his eyes heavenward. He'd known all along it was a pipe dream. They had wasted an hour. He could have been at the hospital with Allie. He started to follow Joe and Harry toward the stairs, but something nudged his mind. He stopped, looking around the cellar. Something he had seen? Clay looked up at the ceiling again, and there it was—an irregular board that didn't quite match the others.

"Hey, wait. Come back here."

The other two turned, looking surprised. Clay pointed. "Up there, see that board?"

Harry peered up. "I don't see anything."

"I do." Joe craned his neck. "I'll betcha there's some reason that board is set in there like that."

Harry could see it now and was almost gibbering in his excitement. "I'll get a ladder."

As soon as he returned with a tall stepladder, Clay climbed up to where he could reach the board. It took a few minutes to work it loose, but eventually he handed it down to Joe and gingerly stuck his hand into the dark cavity. It would be just his luck to grab a brown recluse spider. His groping fingers encountered a smooth surface. Startled, he jerked back.

"Find anything?" Harry asked.

"Maybe." Clay drew out a square wooden box about a foot long and almost that wide. Joe reached up to take it, and Clay descended the ladder.

Harry grabbed for the box, but Joe jerked it back out of reach. "We'll take it upstairs and open it there."

When they reached the kitchen, Joe set the box in the middle of the table and examined it. "Locked."

Harry brought over a heavy butcher knife. "Here. Use this."

Joe inserted the blade under the lid and pried upward. A splintering of wood, and the lock gave. Clay held his breath. Whatever was in that box had already caused the death of three people.

Joe lifted the lid—a flash of brilliance, green, red, and gold. Harry lifted out a necklace with a diamond-and-emerald pendant. "Would you look at that! There's a fortune here."

"And it goes with me," Joe said. He reached for his cell

phone. "I'm calling for an escort. No way am I going to walk out carrying this box by myself."

"While we're waiting for help, why don't we make a list of the items?" Clay suggested.

"Good idea." Harry picked up a notebook from the table. "You name them, I'll write them down."

"Okay, I guess that's all right," Joe agreed. "Start with that necklace."

By the time the backup car arrived, the kitchen table was ablaze with fiery gems. Harry sighed. "I don't even want to know how much all this is worth."

"More than we'll ever see in a lifetime," Clay said.

Joe dismissed them with a contemptuous shrug. "For my money they're not worth the trouble they caused. Four lives ruined over that pile of rocks."

Clay watched as Harry and Joe placed the pieces in the box. Four lives ruined: Otis, Eliza, Maude, and Mary. And Allie had almost been caught in the web. One good thing would come out of all of this: since the mystery had been solved, Allie could open her bed-and-breakfast. She and Cora would be busy making their dream come true. He just hoped there would be room in her life for him.

Allie stood by a window, waiting for Clay to arrive and take her home from the hospital. There he was! She'd been looking forward to this all morning, anxious to get back home.

Home. She examined the word, liking the sound of it. Only a short time ago she had been worried, broke, and uncertain of the future. Now she had friends and a lovely home, and would soon have a new business. She remembered how badly she had wanted to keep the house, and now it was hers. No one could take it away from her. She'd walk out of this emergency room a free woman. With Mary Olson in jail, the last barrier to opening the bed-and-breakfast had been removed. Of course, a new story had been added to the rumors concerning the Ramsdale house. Maude Witner had been murdered there, attacked by a woman crazed over the rumors of stolen jewels.

How could she overcome those stories? Would anyone want to stay in a place where things like that happened?

Finally Clay was there. "Morning. How do you feel?"

"Great. Getting out of the hospital will do that for you."

He laughed. "Let's go, then. You have a welcoming committee waiting for you."

She raised her eyebrows, and he elaborated. "Cora and Harry and Taz."

"Taz." She repeated the name. "It was a lucky day when we found him."

"It sure was. He played a big part in your rescue."

Allie savored the ride home. The colors of the flowers seemed brighter, the sun warmer. There was something about coming so close to death that made life more precious. When they reached the house, she climbed the steps to the porch and walked into Cora's arms.

"Welcome home."

Allie hugged her. "It's wonderful to be here."

Harry waited just inside the door to shake her hand, and in the kitchen the table was set with the best china. A basket of pink roses served as a centerpiece. Allie heard an excited scrabbling of puppy feet against the floorboards. A small black bundle of energy launched himself at her. She caught Taz up in her arms, laughing as he squirmed, trying to lick her face.

"You're a brave little dog, you are."

He barked as if agreeing with her assessment of his character. Allie held him close to her chest, and he nuzzled under her chin. Good, brave, little buddy.

After lunch, while they were still seated around the table, stuffed with Cora's excellent food, Allie thought how blessed she was to have such good friends. Taz lay beside his feed dish, growling occasionally at the remains of the largest steak Clay could find, a reward for his bravery and his dedication to Allie.

Cora broke the silence. "Now there's nothing standing in the way of opening our bed-and-breakfast."

Harry cleared his throat. "Guess you won't want me hanging around anymore after the way I wasn't honest with you."

Allie remembered how hard he had worked on the landscaping, the way he had helped rescue her. Eliza, too, had
been fond of Harry.

She smiled at him. "You're a part of this place, and we're
friends. You have a home here as long as you need it. I think
Eliza would be pleased."

Harry's eyes were moist. "You're a lot like her. A real sweet
lady."

Allie blinked back tears. *Like Eliza?* A few weeks ago she
wouldn't have thought that was much of a compliment. Now
she felt honored by the comparison. Clay had found Eliza's
portrait behind a chest of drawers in the attic and restored it to
its old place over the mantel. Allie allowed herself a contented
sigh. She liked to think Eliza had come home.

Allie inspected the dining room. Tonight she and Cora were
hosting their first dinner party. Her parents were there, Harry,
Clay, and Roger of course. Deke and Bill and their wives were
present and overcome with the good fortune of dining in Miss
Eliza's house. Cora had conducted a guided tour over every
inch of the restored mansion, including the basement.

This was the group of people who had helped them realize
their dream. Next week their guests would start arriving, and
they were booked solid all the way through December.

Deke rose, looking important as he lifted his glass of Cora's
special fruit punch. "I want to make a toast."

They quieted, and he went on. "To Cora and Allie. They've
done a great job on this place, and I know Miss Eliza's somewhere up there looking down and smiling."

"Hear, hear," Bill said, then subsided in embarrassment.

Allie thought of Eliza's commission to clear Otis' name.
They'd not only managed to do that, but Mary Olson was await-
ing trial for the murders of Eliza Ramsdale and Maude Wheeler.

Only one thing remained to make her cup overflow. Clay. That
time she had been in danger of losing her life made her realize
that she loved him, and she had a feeling from things he'd said
and done that he felt the same way. She'd half expected some

sign that he wanted to build a closer relationship, but so far he had been silent.

After dinner, when they had adjourned to the parlor for coffee and conversation, Clay intercepted Allie.

"Come outside for a few minutes. It's a beautiful night."

She glanced toward the parlor, and he intervened. "They'll be all right. Cora will see to everyone's needs."

He held the door open, and she let him usher her out into the spring night. They strolled to the wrought-iron gate at the front of the drive, holding hands. Allie stopped to look back at the house. "It's beautiful."

"Yes, it is, and so are you." He gripped her hands in his. "I'm not trying to rush you into anything, but we've been so busy trying to find out what was going on, we've not really had a chance for us. What do you think about spending some time getting to know each other?"

Allie smiled up at him. Nothing could please her more. "I think it's a wonderful idea."

He put an arm around her shoulders, drawing her close.

"Clay?"

"What?"

"Do you think Eliza would be pleased with all we've done?"

"I think she'd be very pleased. We've restored her home and cleared Otis' name, and you're going to live here, keeping the Ramsdale house in the family."

He turned her to face him. "We've been through a lot together, but I think the best is still ahead of us."

His lips brushed hers, and Allie leaned into his embrace. Meeting Clay was the best thing that could have happened to her. She glanced up at him, lips slightly parted, and he kissed her again, slower and sweeter this time.

The moon showered silver around them, while a black and white puppy watched from the shelter of a lilac bush. The Ramsdale house, clean and bright, restored to its former beauty, stood behind them, and for a moment Allie fancied she felt Eliza's presence, as if she approved and gave them her blessing.